The Light Walker

By Sarah Fenwick

Sarah Fenwick was born in Kenya in 1966 and has a multicultural background with roots in the UK and Cyprus. After studying Journalism at the University of Wisconsin, Sarah wrote for the national media in Nicosia, modern Europe's last divided capital. Sarah covered a wide range of topics from politics to music before moving to Germany, contemporary Europe's first reunified country. The Light Walker is her debut fiction book, and she chose the magical realism genre for its blend of historical facts and imagination.

Other books available on Amazon by Sarah Fenwick

Digital Marketing for Musicians

Transformation Journal

Table of Contents

ISBN: 9798474245119

Imprint: Independently published

www.sarahfenwickauthor.com

Author photo: Savvas Hadjigeorgiou.

Cover art: Sarah Fenwick.

Drawing on page 136: Sarah Fenwick.

Part I

Chapter 1

Alexandros Kyprianides was born in Nicosia on the island of Cyprus in 1940. The family home was in the old city, surrounded by traditional sandstone houses and stately trees which formed shallow, narrow canyons that hid mysterious stories blanketed by humidity and dust.

Stories that whispered and fluttered from mouth to mouth through centuries of history. Stories of injustice and suffering in wars. Tales celebrating births and victories, and myths mourning epic tragedies.

The words floated around, circling one another in endless murmurs, a whirl of discarded shawls around a gypsy's defiant dance.

Nicosia, September 21st, 1950

Nobody had remembered his tenth birthday; it was just another scorching day in class for Alexandros Kyprianides. The sun baked the uninsulated school building in old Nicosia and Alex pulled his tie and collar away from his sweaty neck without making the slightest bit of difference. Another student swatted at a fly which then buzzed around Alex's face, caroming off his ear when he batted at it in irritation.

Alex gritted his teeth and shook his head as he sat through the latest and most egregious of his mathematics teacher's faulty calculations. Mr. Peyton didn't seem capable of finding the correct answers to the problems he set, but Alex had always been too shy to say anything.

Until now – this was too much. He went to the blackboard and crossed out the teacher's solution, replacing it with his own answer.

The other students nudged each other with surprise and glee. Such actions were unheard of, students would never dare to contradict a teacher. Spittle flecked Mr. Peyton's lips, and he turned several shades of outrage as he cuffed Alexandros around the ear. The boy clutched the side of his head as his ear rang and burned.

The teacher pointed to the door. "Get out, you impertinent boy! Go to the headmaster's study immediately."

Alex flinched and hurried out of the classroom, scraping his hand over his bald head. His hair had fallen out when he was young because of a hereditary disease, and it had never grown back. Once there, Alex peered around the head's spartan office from underneath his eyebrows, expecting the worst. But when he dared to meet the man's gaze, he was surprised to see faint smile lines forming around the warm brown eyes looking back at him.

The head asked the boy what had happened, and Alex wrote out his thinking about the maths problem, showing that his solution was the right one. "It's an easy equation," Alex said, "but Mr. Peyton makes mistakes."

The head pursed his lips and blew out a breath, saying: "That's not very respectful, Alexandros, but I see you're a bright boy." He ran his thumb over his chin. "I'm going to send you to the British Council for academic tests. We'll soon learn whether you have more than just a talent for insolence. Off you go home, and mind that you don't correct any more teachers while you're here. It's never too early to learn some discretion."

Alex walked out of the school gates feeling a rising sense of accomplishment and took a deep breath of the warm afternoon air.

"Hey Alex, did you get into trouble?"

He turned and saw a group of boys from his class cycling through the gates. The leader of the gang, Christos, rode up to him and said, "Want to go on a bike ride?"

Alex's cheeks flushed. "I...I don't have a bike."

"Here, you can ride mine." Christos pushed the handlebars of his red, shiny bicycle at Alex. "Get on. Let's see how you ride."

Alex sat on the bicycle and wobbled for a few feet before falling off, scraping his hands on the tarmac with his schoolmates' raucous laughter ringing in his ears. Preferring to study, he'd never learned to ride a bicycle. Alex put his hand in his mouth, sucking on the scraped skin and tasting blood and asphalt almost as bitter as his humiliation.

Christos pushed Alex away from his bike with his foot.

"All those brains and you can't even ride a bike, baldy," he sneered.

The boys mounted their bikes and rode away, and Alex watched with tear-filled eyes. As their blurry silhouettes faded into the shimmering horizon, he muttered, "At least I'm not an idiot."

From then on, Christos and his gang often followed Alex home from school on their bikes, taunting him and kicking him in the shins before riding off with scornful laughs. Alex's jaw burned from the grinding of his teeth in reaction to the bullies and he flinched every time a tall student walked past him, fearing it was Christos.

Several weeks after the incident with the maths teacher, Alex's headteacher called him into his office. "Alexandros, your test scores were amongst the highest ever recorded," he said. "I've spoken with the British Council, and they've agreed to take you on as a special student. You'll train for university exams and improve your English," he said.

"What about school?" Alex said.

"You won't study here anymore. Your classes will be with a maths tutor who works with the British Council. His name is Mr. Georgiades," said the head teacher, his brown eyes warm with a smile. "Mind your manners now and keep the corrections to a minimum."

Alex's eyes filled with tears of relief, and he left school hoping that Christos wouldn't find out where he was going. In fact, he didn't see Christos until several years later when the bully confronted him on a narrow, walled street near the British Council. Alex looked around for an escape but there was nowhere to run as Christos circled Alex on his bright red bicycle. "We heard you joined the British. You're not as smart as you think you are," Christos jeered. "You know what we're going to do to those Englishmen? My father says EOKA will slaughter every single one of them."

The three boys with him laughed. Alex turned to run, but Christos was already on the attack and pushed him to the ground before riding away. The bike swung from side to side between Christos' wiry legs as Alex shrieked at his back.

Suddenly, the road in front of the cyclists appeared to narrow into a sliver. The bullies threw up their arms to protect their faces as the walls closed in on them. Out of control, the bicycles veered and crashed into one another. They ended up in a tangle on the tarmac, looking around in shock at the now perfectly normal appearance of the road. Christos rubbed his face and stared at the blood on his scraped arms.

Alex scrubbed at his naked head with both hands, throwing a troubled look over his shoulder as he walked away.

Nicosia, January 1955.

The acting Governor of Cyprus, Sir James Merin, lived near the British Council where Alex was studying. The governor was deep in thought as he paced and tapped his cane on the stone floor, only looking up when he heard a knock at his office door. The secretary's voice echoed in the high-ceilinged room. "Sorry to disturb, Sir James," his secretary said. "Professor Leo Carter is here for his appointment. Are you ready to meet with him?"

Sir James stopped pacing and tapped his cane on the floor. "It'll have to be quick - I'm expecting the new governor in a little while," he said.

Professor Carter walked past the secretary into the spacious office set inside an elegant two-storey sandstone building. He looked up at the governor and smiled as they shook hands. "Thanks for meeting me, Sir James."

Sir James smiled: "Good to see you here, Leo, no need for the 'sir'. It's been a while. How's Oxford and what brings you to Cyprus?"

"Everything's fine at home. I'm heading a delegation from Oxford to find scientists for the Ministry of Defence, and I wanted to keep you in the loop," Professor Carter said.

Sir James looked taken aback. "Scientists? What on earth for?"

Carter pressed his lips together. "The ministry's been fending off attacks in the colonies. We must find mathematicians to join the staff of GCHQ. They're expanding the military analysts' department," he said.

"Ah yes, ex-Bletchley Park, the code breakers. I know the director," Sir James said.

"The director's the one who sent me to see you," Carter said.

The governor frowned. "How can I help? We're under a lot of pressure here ourselves from EOKA militants. I don't have time for much else," he said.

"I understand, of course. I'm appealing for your influence. The British Council might know of mathematicians at the level we need them."

"Indeed, they might. And what of it?" Sir James snapped.

Carter put a sheet of paper on the desk. "These are the exam results we're looking for. Genius level. With your help, we could find out if there are any candidates in Cyprus."

Sir James crossed his arms. "Can't you deal with it yourself, Leo? I don't have time to run around looking for your child prodigies when EOKA is breathing down our necks."

Carter took a deep breath. "Well, with your permission, I'll visit the British Council and speak with the head there," he said. "The ministry will sponsor the promising candidates. We'll bring them to Oxford so I can train them in advanced mathematics. The ministry will reimburse us, of course."

Sir James rubbed his forehead. "Yes, I don't see why not."

Carter let out a short, sharp breath. "Thank you. When he arrives in England, you won't have to worry about the candidates, if we find any, that is. I'll supervise their studies and keep them occupied."

"Let the ministry know I'll help in any way I can. Pass on my best to the director," Sir James said.

The men parted with a final handshake and the governor's secretary made an appointment for Carter at the British Council for the next day. The British Council's staff was in a flurry of preparations for the exam period when Carter arrived. A flustered librarian greeted him.

"I know I'm early. Don't make a fuss, please. Is the director ready to meet with me?" Carter said.

The librarian bobbed her head and led him to a large office which smelled of book leather, paper, and a blanket of hushed, still air. Dan Trennings was standing by his desk and rushed to shake Carter's hand.

"Please sit down, Professor Carter."

"Good morning, Dan. I won't take much of your time," Carter said, taking a seat in one of the comfortable leather chairs.

"So, what can I do for you?" Trennings said.

Carter placed a paper with test scores on the desk. "The governor's given me permission to look for exceptional minds, especially mathematicians. Do you have any students with these test scores?" he said.

Dan Trennings looked at the list of scores. "We have one possible candidate, a student called Alexandros Kyprianides. He would easily reach those levels," he said.

Carter straightened his back. "Here, at the British Council?" he said, focusing an intense gaze on Trennings.

"Yes, professor. He's studying mathematics. Alexandros has an astonishing mind."

"What else can you tell me about him? Does he speak English?" Carter said.

"Yes. We've been working on his English. He's fluent enough when he chooses to speak it," Trennings said.

"What do you mean? He prefers Greek?"

"No, I mean he prefers not to speak at all. He's shy. Maybe because he's bald."

"Bald?"

"His hair fell out when he was five years old from a rare condition."

Professor Carter stroked his thumb over the back of his hand, the only sign the news had taken him aback. "Why's he studying here and not in school?" he said.

"Alexandros is a bit of a misfit in terms of the standard educational system." Trennings said. "He's simply too advanced. He corrected his teacher on an equation in front of the whole class when he was ten years old."

Carter shook his head, and a reluctant smile twitched his lips. "The lad is either foolhardy or brave," he said.

Trennings shrugged. "I'm not sure which one he is. Anyway, to the head's credit, he sent the student to us for further testing."

"And how did he perform in his tests here? Is he ready for university courses?" Professor Carter said.

"Yes, he passed the university level entrance exams in maths with flying colours when he was only 12 years old," Trennings said.

"Can you give me his tutor's address? I want to meet him," Carter said.

Trennings looked over at his secretary, who wrote down the address on a piece of paper and gave it to Professor Carter.

Carter stood up to leave. "One more thing. I need you to offer a grant to Alexandros' parents on our behalf allowing us to take him to England. I'll train him in advanced mathematics at Oxford." Carter turned to the door. "Could you arrange that as soon as possible with the boy's father, please, and let the governor's secretary know when it's confirmed. The governor's expecting to hear from you."

Trennings nodded. "Okay, I'll see what I can do by tomorrow," he said.

A few days after Professor Carter's visit to the British Council, Alexandros' father, Nikos, swaggered into Trennings' office. He looked around at the bookshelves with little respect in his eyes. Trenning's nose wrinkled as Nikos sat down and leaned back in his chair. His shirt buttons strained across an ample belly and the stale smell of sweat, garlic and cigarettes filled the closed space.

Nikos tilted his chin up and drew on his cigarette, glaring at Trennings through the pungent smoke. "Why did you bring me here?" Nikos said, His lungs rasping and wheezing as he dragged on the cigarette.

Trennings coughed on his way to open a window. "I have an offer for you, Mr. Kyprianides. The ministry is ready to give your son a scholarship and pay for his education so he can study in Oxford."

Nikos crossed his arms. "So? What do you want from me? I don't even have the money to feed my family."

Trennings pursed his lips. "You're the boy's father. We need your permission to take Alexandros abroad," he said.

Nikos leaned forward; eyes gleaming: "What's in it for me?"

"Money, a monthly allowance," Trennings said.

"How much?"

"We can offer you 15 pounds a month."

Nikos sat back and folded his arms again. "No. I want 20 pounds a month. Otherwise, I'll send him out to work in the asbestos mines. We need the money."

Trenning's fists clenched on the desk. "Be reasonable, Mr. Kyprianides, it must be obvious to you that Alexandros wouldn't last a day in the mines."

Nikos sneered and dug his hands into his pockets, turning them inside out. "Pay me what I want if you need him so much. You are a rich Englishman and I have nothing but empty pockets."

Trennings sighed. He thrust a paper and some money across his desk. "Have it your way, Mr. Kyprianides. 20 pounds a month, it is. Here's the first payment. Sign the contract and you can take the money."

Nikos signed his name with a thumbprint and grabbed the cash, thrusting it deep into his pocket. "I'll be back the same time next month," he said as he left, fumbling with his trousers.

Ermou Street, Nicosia

On most days, Alex sat at his tutor's desk, poring over complex equations with intense concentration, his nose almost touching the papers as he read them. The winters in Nicosia can be bone-chilling, so that night, his tutor's wife had wrapped Alex up in a navy-blue sweater and a grey cap to keep his bald head warm.

Suddenly, the front door of the tiny house on Ermou Street opened, letting in a rush of cool, rainy air. Professor Carter walked into the room wearing a dark suit and hat and carrying a briefcase. Carter's heavy-lidded eyes took in the small room, and he jutted his chin in Alex's direction, expecting him to stand up.

17

Alex ignored him, too engrossed in his work. Mr. Georgiades glared at his student and tapped him on the shoulder, urging him to stand up in respect. But Alex hunched over as if to escape inside his own body, a habit he'd formed after Christos' bullying.

Knowing the boy's fear of strangers, Mr. Georgiades poked him again. "Stand up, Alexandros, what are you afraid of? Professor Carter only wants to talk to you," he said.

Alex finally staggered to his feet, knees knocking against each other as the backs of his legs bumped into the chair. At 15 years old, Alex was a gawky, gangly boy and his legs were bony, as were his hands and arms. Almond-shaped brown eyes were narrowed into slits from reading so much and his jawline was prominent beneath sunken cheeks, making him look several years older than he actually was.

Carter tilted his head. "Your teacher tells me that you're a brilliant mathematician, Alexandros," he said.

The tutor's speech quickened. "He's only 15 years old, professor and he already solves some of the most difficult problems in mathematics."

Alex lowered his eyes and stared at his papers.

"Look at me, lad. There's no need to be afraid. I'm not here to hurt you. On the contrary, we've decided to grant you a scholarship to study at Oxford," Carter said in a calm tone. "I've agreed on everything with Mr. Georgiades and your parents and I promise it'll change your life. You'll soon come and study with me and work for the British government afterwards."

Carter smiled at Alex. "Buck up, lad. This is good news for your family because the government will cover the cost of your expenses and pay your parents and Mr. Georgiades here a salary. Do you have any questions?" he said.

The silence drew out. Mr. Georgiades broke the spell when he prodded Alex's shoulder again. "Speak up, Alexandros. This is a great honour. The British government will take care of you for life. You'll never have to worry about an income. You should be grateful to help your parents."

Alex sat back down and looked at his maths book while the men talked in an undertone for a few more minutes. Professor Carter left, clicking the door shut behind him and letting cold fresh air into the room once again. Alex's shoulders relaxed as he concentrated on solving problems, ignoring his tutor's impatient gaze. He put his hands together in the prayer position and looked at his tutor. "Seven, one, two, one, seven," he said.

Mr Georgiades tutted. "Another one? That's the third today, Alexandros." He walked seven steps to the kitchen, lifted out one plate from the cabinet, then took two slices of bread and one piece of ham. After seven strides back to the table, the portly tutor handed Alex his sandwich, muttering under his breath: "A mathematical genius, yes. Clueless about everything else. Wouldn't even eat if I didn't get his food for him."

Mr. Georgiades' chubby cheeks creased into dimples as he watched Alex work contentedly on his equations, sandwich in hand. The art of mathematics was his student's sole source of happiness and he found it difficult to communicate in any other way. The tutor's eyes turned sad when he thought of the rejections Alex had faced from his peers. Children can be contemptuous and mean if they sense that someone is different to them.

Day by day, Alex and Mr. Georgiades had grown closer, and the boy had grown to trust his tutor. His abilities had developed faster than his teacher could hope for, even knowing his natural skills. Now that the lad was out of his schoolmates' reach, Mr. Georgiades' only worry was Alex's parents.

Alex's family home, Nicosia.

Alex's family lived near Ermou Street on another narrow road lined by one-storey terraced dwellings. The homes were so close to each other it was difficult to tell where one started and the other ended. Not long after his encounter with Professor Carter, his mother, Maria, confronted him in his bedroom early in the morning, before he'd had the chance to escape to his tutor's house.

The penetrating odours of garlic, onions and bay leaves followed his mother around, she always seemed to be cooking and the aromas of her dishes permeated the house. Maria sat on the bed which groaned under her weight, sinking by half a metre. Five rolls of stomach fat pushed against her smock, one on top of the other like tyres. It was a sight Alex never got tired of watching and he smiled when his mother caught his eye, shaking her hand in a mock warning.

"Don't you make fun of your mama. Nobody asked me if it was okay for you to go to England," she said. Maria sighed and gave Alex an anxious look. "When will you be going? What about the costs? How will we pay for everything?"

Alex shrugged and avoided her eyes as he fidgeted with a cold metal ruler and looked at the maths problem in front of him. Maria beckoned him over and pressed a cap over his bald head. His family couldn't afford wood for the fireplace that winter and they faced a long, chilly winter season. Alex pulled away from her as she fussed with his cap and Maria's forehead creased. "Oh! What a fine son I've got. You can't even talk to your mother," she said. "What am I going to do with you? Since the day you were born, maths, only maths!"

"Shut up, woman. I don't want to listen to your non-stop nonsense. Blah, blah, blah!" his father bellowed from the other room.

"But how are we going to make ends meet?" Maria said.

Alex covered his ears against the shouts and rocked back and forth to ease the pain in his ears. Recently, his parents had been fighting more than usual, and his hearing was sensitive. Alex could hear a car door opening in the next street and loud noises nearby quickly overwhelmed him. But his acute hearing was a matter of indifference to his parents, who fought at the tops of their lungs and never noticed Alex's sensitivity. The boy's father often scolded him for being too soft and shouted even louder if he saw Alex flinching or covering his ears.

"The ministry will pay for it all," Nikos said. "The money has already started coming in and Alex will stay in a rich house in Oxford. I've arranged everything with Georgiades. Will you shut up?" Nikos yelled.

Maria wrung her hands. "He's only 15 years old, Nikos!" she said. "Other than maths, what can he do? What if something goes wrong with his studies. What if they throw him out of their house? How will he survive?"

"For the last time, Maria, shut up, or else!"

Alex's eyes opened wide, and he looked at his mother in mute pleading with his hands raised in prayer. If she didn't stop talking, his father would hit her and pinch her arms and Alex couldn't bear it when she cried. But tears were already streaming down Maria's cheeks, dripping onto her chin and her grey, food-stained smock. She rocked and puffed her way heavily to her feet. As the mattress rose, the springs squeaked, pinged, and sighed in relief.

Alex forgot his father's threats and yelling as he stared at his mother. He was busy calculating how long it would take her to reach the kitchen door, quickly factoring in the distance, her weight, and speed. Precisely 59 seconds and 15 steps later, her broad back lumbered through the kitchen door. Alex checked his watch and frowned. Why was there one second under his calculation of 60 seconds? He hated imprecision and trusted entirely in the power of mathematics. His forehead smoothed over as he quickly recalculated, remembering his mother had lost a kilo because of another one of her many attempts to diet. That explained how she'd beaten his time.

Nikos' slap rocked his face to the right and wrenched his neck. Alex's eyes watered at the dank smell of Nikos' cigarette-laden breath. "Do as you're told, otherwise I'll send you to the mines," Nikos said.

Maria waddled back into Alex's room and threw herself at Nikos. "Leave him alone!" she screamed.

Nikos had a corded squat body built up over a lifetime in construction work and when he threw his weight against Maria, the air exploded out of her lungs as she hit the wall. Nikos snarled in her face. "He's leaving in two days. If I hear another word out of either of you, you know what will happen."

Chapter 2

After spending his childhood years living in a small town, the massive, wallowing sea made Alex feel insignificant. In ten leaden steps, he'd boarded the British warship to England, headed for the unknown.

The rocking waves made him seasick, so studying maths was a problem. Instead, he soothed his fears by counting to himself. When the seasickness had passed, he emerged on the ship's deck, the fresh mineral smell of the salt air clearing his head.

The crew of the warship was curious about the boy on the deck who sat on his own for hours just staring at the waves. One crew member asked if he was okay but soon retreated in the face of Alex's abstracted gaze. They left him alone after that, although the cook made sure he had regular meals and ginger tea to counteract his seasickness.

On the third day at sea, Professor Carter sat next to him wearing a luxurious, soft, dark suit. The professor didn't seem concerned about the way Alex's shoulders instantly started hunching and he made a soothing motion with his hands.

"Don't worry, lad, I won't harm you. My name is Leonardo Pisano, but my friends call me Fibonacci," he said.

Alex stopped shrinking into himself, smirked and shook his head 'no'.

"Ha, caught me, did you?" Carter said. "Well done lad. Fibonacci died a long time ago. It's just my little joke. Do you remember me? I'm a great admirer of Fibonacci's work, aren't you?"

Alex came alive with vigorous energy, jabbing his finger at the deck of the ship. Professor Carter looked up to see a shimmering figure that appeared to be the richly dressed medieval mathematician, Leonardo Pisano Fibonacci. The apparition vanished as quickly as it had appeared.

"Zero, one, one, two, three, five, eight," Alex said, smiling and waving his hands as he reverted to math-speak.

Carter paled but he recovered quickly after brushing off the apparition as a figment of his imagination. He smiled back at Alex. "Well done. You know your Fibonacci numbers," Carter said. "My real name is Professor Leo Carter. You can call me Leo. Governor Merin asked me to look in on you to make sure you're alright. I heard good things about you at the British Council."

Leo's smiling, heavy-lidded eyes connected with Alex's narrowed dark brown ones. "What's the eighth number in the Fibonacci Sequence?" he said.

"Thirteen," Alex said.

"Only if…"

"You start from zero."

"Well done, boy, so you can talk. You'll stay at the governor's home for a few days until I'm back in Oxford," Leo said, but Alex was staring at the sea, back in his familiar trance.

"What are you doing, lad? Counting waves with Fibonacci sequences?" Leo said.

Alex nodded dreamily and Leo smiled to himself. As he left, the professor placed a card next to Alex, making sure not to touch him on the instinct that he wouldn't like it. "This is my visiting card in case you need it. I'll see you soon," he said. His only answer was a brisk gust of wind sprinkling sea spray around his head, and Leo walked away with a slight smile on his face.

Oxford

After his long journey from Cyprus, Alex stood outside Sir James's family home, feeling bone weary. Imposing marble columns towered over him as he walked past them towards the front door of a graceful mansion.

A dark pond was to his left, partially hidden by trees and surrounded by a recently mowed, expansive lawn. He could smell freshly cut green grass along with the decaying, mossy scent of brackish pondwater.

Alex touched the doorbell and the door was flung open, interrupting the chiming bell. A young woman stood in the doorway in a flurry of blonde hair and irritation. Her blue eyes glared spikes of spite at him and narrowed in contempt. "Who are you, and what are you doing here without an invitation?" she snapped.

Alex stuck his chin firmly into his chest, making his muffled answer impossible to understand.

"Mother!" yelled the contemptuous young woman. She turned on her heel and flounced away, white-blonde hair snapping at her shoulders and high-heeled shoes cracking on the shiny marble floor.

A tall, slim woman in her early forties walked to the door, periwinkle eyes softening when she saw Alex looking up at her like a dog who'd just been told off for peeing on the carpet. Alex automatically counted 63 white roses embroidered on her long, pale pink dress. The woman touched her pearl necklace. "You must be my husband's protégé from Cyprus, Alexandros. Come in. I'm Willow. Did Regina frighten you? She's - well, she is who she is, there's no need to take it to heart," she said.

Willow led him past an elegant marble staircase to a small room at the back of the house and on the left of a cavernous kitchen. Someone had shoved a narrow bed against the back wall and a small wooden desk took up the corner of the room. Covered in plain white sheets and a grey blanket, the bed offered a cool welcome as Alex sat on it, the freshly laundered woollen blanket scratching against the back of his legs.

Willow turned to leave. "Meals are at midday and 6 pm and you'll eat your food in your room. Your mathematics tutor will come in a few days," she said. "Study hard and don't disturb anyone else. While you're here, stay away from Regina and her brother. Spare me the arguments." Willow softened her words with a slight smile.

Alex looked at the floor and counted to five. By the time he'd peeked up from under his eyebrows, Willow had gone, leaving a trace of rose perfume lingering in the air.

He had little to unpack and it took him less than 10 minutes to settle into his new room. With nothing else to do, he took out one of his maths books and started studying. At 4 pm, one of the staff called him to come to the kitchen next door. They were serving an afternoon tea break and he accepted the tray with a pot of steaming tea and chocolate biscuits with shaking hands. It'd been hours since he'd last eaten.

"Where do you come from, then?" one of the kitchen maids said.

Alex didn't answer her and was too shy to look her in the eyes.

"My name's Emily. Mind you bring that tray back," she said.

Other than the maid's passing interest, the rest of the staff ignored him. Alex walked back to his room, hoping it would stay that way.

Several days after his arrival in Oxford, the smell of slow-cooked poultry and fresh bread filtered into his room. Alex heard panicked, shouted instructions echoing through the kitchen and the clash and clang of pots and pans set his nerves on edge. He covered his hyper-sensitive ears and curled up on the bed.

"Truss that turkey right, you idiot. The governor's here, and he'd better be happy with his meal," the cook shouted.

There was a rap at the door and Alex scrambled to his feet, putting his back against the wall of the narrow room before Emily's gentle voice soothed him. "Are you there? The governor wants you to eat dinner with the family. We're serving in five minutes," she said.

Alex's stomach knotted and he counted the 25 steps to the dining room as slowly as he could, watching his shoes reflected on the polished marble floor. As he entered the dining room, he saw Sir James sitting at a long, formal table covered with a fine, white linen tablecloth. Willow was to his right and Regina glowered from her seat to his left. The governor pointed to the chair next to Regina. "Sit here, lad," he said.

Alex subsided into the chair and stared at his blue China plate with polished sterling silver forks, spoons and knives lined up in an order he didn't understand. He counted five fork clinks and stared at the candlelight glimmering along a line of crystal wine glasses. What if something broke when he touched it?

The rich, savoury smell of hot chicken soup wafted from his plate and saliva filled his mouth. Still, he didn't dare pick up one of the two spoons next to his plate and the silence drew out in the tense atmosphere.

"He doesn't talk very much. You'd never know this boy has the finest mathematical mind we've ever come across," Sir James said.

Willow smoothed her hair. "It's true, darling. He barely says a word to anyone. We hardly notice he's here," she said.

Regina scoffed. "But Daddy, are you sure he's a genius? He doesn't seem in the least bit dazzling to me," she said. Her sarcastic laugh hung in the air for three milliseconds before the scraping of a chair drowned it out and Regina's twin brother, Oliver, plonked himself on a chair. As tall and blond as his sister, his eyes were as sullen as an overcast day as he glowered at Alex.

"What's he doing here? I thought he had to stay in his room during mealtimes. He's not even civilized," Oliver said.

"Stop it, you two," Sir James snapped. "You're 20 years old and haven't accomplished a single thing in your lives. You're spoiled rotten, thanks to your mother. The boy's here to stay for a few days. He's a sight more intelligent than both of you put together. Eat and be quiet!"

Oliver bit his lip, looking at Regina with red-rimmed eyes. The siblings narrowed their eyes at each other like jealous cats and almost hissed.

Willow tutted. "Now, now, children, let's have a nice meal for once," she said, raising her chin and peering at Alex. "As long as he keeps to himself, he can stay."

"It's not your place to say who stays or goes, Willow. He's a British government asset," Sir James huffed. "You'll take care of him as I see fit. The boy is staying here for king and country. He's not a bloody houseguest."

Willow stared at her food. "Yes - I apologize, my dear."

Sir James grunted and started eating. Everyone else followed suit in silence until Alex suddenly jerked his hand and tipped over his plate. The crash of his soup plate hitting the ground shattered the silence. Alex yelped as hot soup spilled onto his lap. It wasn't the only thing burning his legs.

Underneath the table, Regina had pinched and twisted the skin on his upper thigh with sincere viciousness.

Sir James looked up from his food, frowning. "What's the fuss about this time? Can't any of you sit still?" he said, pointing to the door. "Go to your room and finish your meal there, lad. Mind you learn some manners."

Alex scurried to the door; shoulders hunched. He lurched over Oliver's outstretched foot on his way out and fell on the marble floor. The soup on his trousers made the floor wet and his shoes were slippery, making him scrabble like a crab on ice when he tried to get up. Oliver reached out his hand to help Alex up but withdrew it at the last second with a sneer while Regina tittered at his predicament, flicking a crumb off her silk dress with a sharply manicured nail. The twins smirked at each other.

Sir James rapped his cane on the floor and glared at his children. "That's enough of that nonsense! You'll mind your manners, the pair of you, or leave the dinner table."

A sudden thunderous rumble came from the far corner of the room, and everyone turned around to see what was happening. The walls *waved* and *rippled* as if they'd turned into a waterfall, going back to their customary solidity and stillness milliseconds later. While they were distracted, Alex hurried out of the dining room to hide in his room.

Willow's hand worried at her collarbone. "What on earth was that sound?" she said.

Oliver's voice was tight. "Why do you prefer him over me?" he whined. Regina tried to catch Oliver's eyes, but they were downcast, and she curled her lip when she saw tears trickling down his cheeks.

The governor harrumphed around his soup as Willow tutted in vain at her children. Nobody remarked on the wall's sudden change of state, and the family finished the meal in their usual silence.

Spheres

The kitchen staff grew more friendly towards Alex after the twins' cruel treatment. Emily was near his age and was especially protective, bringing him treats from the kitchen every morning and afternoon.

"Your maths tutor is here," Emily said the day after the dinner debacle. She tidied up some books and placed his hot tea on the small desk. Leo stood in the doorway and winked at Alex to be rewarded with one of his rare, incandescent smiles.

"Hello Alex! It's Leo Carter. Remember me from the sea voyage? I told you you'd see me again."

"Hello, Fibonacci," Alex said with a sly look in his eyes.

"Ha! A joke. I bet you don't make many of those, Alexandros," Leo said.

Alex blinked at the sound of his own name. Everyone he had met in England seemed to think his name was 'boy'. Leo's heavy-lidded brown eyes smiled warmly into Alex's. For a moment, the meagre English sunlight seemed to brighten up the room.

"You'll be moving to my house in a few days. I live a stone's throw away. Now, let's get to work," Leo said, tapping the pile of books he was carrying with his knuckle.

Excitement flared in Alex's almond-brown eyes at the prospect of studying maths at last. From then on, Leo taught him every day and his small desk filled up with notebooks and textbooks. Alex began to look forward to the endless hours in the Merin's mansion and for the first time since he'd arrived in England, he felt at home.

About a week into their studies, Leo leaned forward in his chair, his glasses misting over from the steam rising from a fragrant pot of Earl Grey tea. Leo gestured to Alex to pick up his pencil and take notes, but a tap at the door interrupted whatever he was going to say and Willow walked in with graceful, elegant movements as Leo stood up to take her hand.

"Willow, it's good to see you," he said.

Willow raised an eyebrow and snapped her hand back with a quick smile. "Is it, Leo? I noticed you didn't come to find me and say hello," she said.

Leo looked at her with a teasing expression. "Was it such a long way for you to come from the living room to see me?" he said.

Willow rolled her eyes. "Anyway, I came to see if you need anything. Tea, perhaps?"

"No, thank you. Emily brought us some earlier," Leo said.

She played with her pearl necklace. "Fine, then. Is Alexandros working hard?" she said.

"Yes, he's doing well, Willow. It's kind of you to ask."

Willow turned to go. "Take care, Leo."

Leo walked the two paces to the door with her. "You too, my lady."

Leo sat down and reopened his book. "Alex, have you heard of the Poincaré Conjecture?"

Alex nodded.

"Tell me about the crucial question in the problem."

"How is the inside of a solid sphere structured in four dimensions or more?" Alex said.

"Yes. I want you to imagine the Earth in space. It's a solid sphere, correct?" Leo said.

Alex nodded.

"Poincaré wanted to understand the internal structure of a solid sphere like a planet. Why do you think that is?" Leo said.

"So that we can understand how all spheres take up space and dimension," Alex said.

Leo sat back. "How do you know this?" he said.

Alex shrugged. "I just know it."

"You must have read it somewhere. Have you tried to solve the problem?" Leo said.

"Not yet."

Leo leaned forward in his chair. "Think about it. If we knew the internal dimensions of a solid sphere, what could we do with them?" he said.

Alex clenched his prominent jaw and pointed to the ceiling. When Leo looked up, there was a giant sphere hanging in space, rotating slowly. Leo found himself on his feet in astonishment. "How do you do that? What are these illusions?"

"The light, I shape the light. It's quicker than talking," Alex said.

Leo sank back into his chair, mouth agape. "Okay, tell me about that later. For now, go on with the problem," he said.

Alex looked at the suspended spheres. "If we knew how to calculate a sphere's internal dimensions, we could understand if our universe was spherical by using the formula and our location in space."

"And what would that mean mathematically?" Leo said.

Alex waved his hand at the rotating sphere and it disappeared inside another, larger sphere. "We could understand how big the sphere of our universe is. We'd be able to calculate whether it's inside another universe," he said.

Leo's eyes were goggling but he took a deep breath and carried on. "Well done. That's a clear analysis. Do you have any other thoughts about this problem?"

Alex waved his hand gently, multiplying the number of spheres inside the main one. "Every sphere inside us could be part of the spheres outside us," he said.

"What do you mean, Alexandros?"

"Mathematical laws connect and change matter. A sphere seems solid, but it's really made of particles and waves," Alex said, moving his hand again. Another sphere appeared next to the first one and both orbs suddenly rippled out into waves like the dining room wall had done a few nights earlier. The waves radiated out from each sphere and connected with a strange, fluting music.

Leo's eyes widened again, but he kept his cool this time. "What would happen if a sphere behaved like a wave instead of a particle with mass?" he said.

Alex gestured towards the orbs. "If a sphere within me changes from a solid particle to a wave, it would connect to another sphere somewhere else in the universe."

"But what if each sphere is closed off to the others?" Leo said.

Alex moved his hand again, one sphere became solid, and the waves of the other sphere fused into it. "Waves behave differently to particles. Waves from one sphere could connect with waves in another closed sphere without damaging it," he said.

Leo's eyes brightened. "I see what you've done there. You've combined theories from Max Planck's quantum field work and Poincare's work on the inner structure of spheres. Aren't they two different things?" he said.

"It depends. Are we thinking like waves or like particles?" Alex said.

Leo guffawed so hard that he had to walk around the room five times. Alex cocked his head and widened his eyes at his professor, which only made him laugh even more.

"Alex, you've just hit on one of life's greatest truths. It's not *what* you look at, it's *how* you look at it that counts," Leo said.

Later that afternoon, Alex and Leo were studying when they heard the crunch of gravel beneath tyres. When Alex rushed to look out of the window, he saw ten Austin Champ military vehicles drawing up outside the mansion. Even over the sound of the gravel, Alex's hearing was sharp enough to overhear Emily telling the cook: "The guvnor's going back to Cyprus. There's trouble there."

"Are you listening to me, Alex?" Leo said, pointing to the maths book.

"Sorry! Someone's coming," Alex said as rapid footsteps approached and Sir James knocked briefly as he strode into the room. At once, Alex hunched over his books and looked down at the desk as the memory of the dinner came rushing back to him.

Leo held out his hand. "You're in a rush, James. Has something happened?"

Sir James shook Leo's hand and tapped his cane on the floor. "I'm leaving for Cyprus today. Keep me informed about the lad's progress. The ministry sent word that they urgently need mathematicians, there's no time left to waste," he said.

"He's doing very well so far. May I ask why you're going?" Leo said.

"We've heard rumours of an imminent uprising in the colony. I'm going over to advise the new governor on nipping it in the bud," Sir James said. "The last thing we need is trouble in Cyprus. The place is like a stick of dynamite next to an open flame."

Leo nodded. "Turkey is the flame, of course. Is it a flying visit?" he said.

"Yes, I'll only be there for a short while. It's time to take the boy to your house, please," Sir James said.

Leo rubbed the back of his neck. "Yes, he'll move in with me tomorrow. If it's not too much to ask, please arrange a message to Mr. Georgiades. He'd appreciate knowing Alex is managing well in England," he said.

Sir James was already on his way out but turned and gave Leo a quick nod. A few minutes later, gravel crunched and pinged underneath the military vehicles as they left. Alex's shoulders stayed hunched over his crossed arms and his eyes were gloomy.

"Don't worry, lad, it'll be okay. The governor will handle everything," Leo said.

But Alex shook his head and refused to take his eyes off the floor, so Leo ended the lesson for the day after coaxing his student into getting some rest. "Try to relax, Alexandros. I'll see you tomorrow for our usual lesson and then you'll come home with me," he said on his way out the door.

Leo's home was just down the lane, and he fretted about Alex on the walk back. Despite his fierce intelligence and talent for mathematics, Alex was fragile and young. He'd have to learn how to look out for himself, but for the time being, Leo felt responsible for him. For a moment, he had such a strong foreboding that he stopped walking to collect himself. Leo leaned against a fence and brushed off the premonition with the thought that Alex would soon be safe and sound under his roof.

Chapter 3

That night, Alex shot up in his bed when he heard Regina tittering outside his door at 3 am. His stomach clenched when there was an answering snicker from Oliver. Alex scrambled into a corner of the room as Regina opened the door. The twins stalked toward him as he shrank back into the wall. He covered his head with his arms as Regina loomed over him and grabbed him by the ear to lift him up.

Oliver twisted his arm high up on his back. "I'll teach you to play favourites with my father. Who do you think you are, you Cypriot peasant?"

Regina bared her teeth. "It's your fault Daddy had to go back to that horrible island! Why aren't you there with all the other rabble? It's your countrymen who are causing all this trouble," she hissed.

Oliver pushed him towards the bedroom door while Regina pulled and twisted his ears. Alex cried out at the pain.

"Nobody's here to protect you. You're about to pay for everything now," Oliver whispered.

As they pushed and pulled at Alex, his nightshirt ripped open. The moonlight came through the window and his skin shone in the dark room. Regina stared at his milky white chest.

Her bloodlust was palpable in her flared nostrils and dilated pupils. She let out an eerie chortle.

"Oliver, this creature makes me think of a disgusting dog. I want to play our game," she said.

Oliver gave an answering snicker. He put a dog collar on Alex. The twins yanked the leash, pulling his light body easily along the corridor. As they walked, they didn't notice the walls rippling like waves in their wake. They also didn't see Emily, who followed them as they forced Alex outside. Regina snickered again as they dragged him towards the pond in the shadowy garden. Alex screamed silently in terror. His mouth was agape, eyes vacant. Emily's cheeks were streaked with tears as she hid behind a tree. If she was to help Alex, she'd have to stay out of sight and wait.

Regina sneered. "I told you he's an idiot. He's gone completely mad. He's revolting!" she said as they reached the pond. Oliver plunged Alex's head into the cold pond and held him down for long moments before pulling at the leash to drag his head out of the water. Each time they yanked his head out of the water, the ghastly twins laughed in Alex's face.

The brackish taste of pond water filled his mouth. His lungs were in agony as he struggled to breathe. At the fourth ducking, Alex's eyes widened in surprise. An air bubble had formed spontaneously around his head, holding its shape long enough for him to take a quick breath. The water flowed around the air bubble, and he took a second breath before it dissolved. Another air bubble quickly replaced the first one, keeping him alive. The elements in the water were changing their state to help him breathe but Alex was in far too much pain to marvel at the miracle.

His tormentors were howling with laughter. As they shrieked and tittered, they didn't notice that the air and water were protecting Alex from drowning. Finally, Oliver dropped the leash. Bored with the torture, the twins turned and walked back into the house. Alex lay face down in the water with air bubbles slithering around his head. He heard Regina sniggering from a long way away before he passed out for the last time.

Chapter 4

Alex opened his eyes and mouth in a silent scream. He'd woken up in a strange room and looked around in panic before fixating on the wallpaper. It was brown with bright green ivy patterns. Leo stood in front of him, holding a glass of water. Alex stared at the water with fear-struck eyes and the professor made a soothing hand gesture. "Calm down, lad. You're safe at my house," he said.

Alex blinked at him with tears pouring down his face. Leo didn't dare touch the boy, not even to comfort him because he was too frightened and on the verge of bolting. Leo sat down on a comfortable chair in a corner of the room.

"The kitchen maid, Emily brought me to you. She ran up the lane to my house in the middle of the night, shaking like a leaf," Leo said. "She saw the twins attacking you and by the time I got there you were unconscious. I had to carry you back home."

Alex wiped away his tears with the back of his hand, then hunched his shoulders and fell asleep. Leo shook his head and muttered to himself. "Bad seeds, those two, bad seeds. That poor boy. Thank goodness I live nearby. Heaven knows what would have happened next. He could have died."

Alex slept and dreamed of walking through time and beyond, travelling around myriad stars and planets on a journey where he experienced space and super novae, walked around spiralling diamond galaxies, and floated in ethereal universes and black holes. Dark matter resonated through him and around him at the same time as whorls of brightly coloured gas circled him. Meteors barrelled silently past as he walked on thin air.

Celestial music broke the silence every so often, and Alex felt his spirit break free as he drifted, his soul becoming one with infinity. He saw his own giant body walking toward him using planets as steppingstones and in the next moment, he was microscopically small, so small he fell through a green planet in a millisecond, so enormous, he was the green planet. His consciousness slipped through the spaces between the universe's atoms as Alex followed an empty path in space-time that only he knew.

He met just one other being on the way, a multi-coloured light being who shimmered and glimmered as it stood suspended in space, a rainbow light spectrum flickering around its gossamer form. The being was simultaneously in front of him and all around him. "You must keep walking the Earth," it mind spoke.

"Why?" Alex mind spoke.

"You are one of one. We are the One. We balance the multi-verses."

"What do you mean?"

"The One is spirit particles with power over energy and matter. There is always one of us on Earth, keeping the balance. You are us."

"Is that why I know things?"

"Yes."

"They hurt me."

"No one will ever hurt you again."

"What's your name?"

"Think of me as Hzartanek, bringer of harmony."

"What's my name?"

"You are Phos, the Light Walker."

"Are there many of us?"

"Many is not a term we understand. We are all and nothing."

"And I'm all and nothing?"

"For now, your energy is in one place, what you call your body. You also exist in multiple dimensions simultaneously."

"I'm afraid, exposed," Alex mind spoke.

A ball of shimmering light appeared in front of Hzartanek. The light floated over to Alex and hovered in front of his mouth.

"Swallow this. It will protect you for all your human days in a state of solid matter. If you need us, touch your heart. The One will help you," Hzartanek mind spoke.

The luminescent ball flowed down Alex's throat and entered his heart as his body vanished into a blinding flash of light.

"Now, Phos, keep walking," Hzartanek mind spoke.

In that second, Alex woke up and looked around the room. The ivy pattern on the brown wallpaper seemed more vivid than before. He got up and walked out of the professor's house. Halfway down the lane, his feet floated off the ground. Alex glided on draughts of air towards a nearby forest and walked for three hours through the woods, stepping between the treetops. Eventually, he fell asleep under a tree, only waking up when the chirping, chiding birds chittered nearby just before dawn. Alex went back to his room so early that the professor never even knew he'd been gone. The Light Walker's first walking quest was in the green English countryside where he started learning about the mysteries of consciousness.

Later that day, Alex and Leo were sitting at a table in the living room near a bay window overlooking the professor's garden. With spring just around the corner, the garden was gradually coming back to life and Alex had reluctantly agreed to leave his room to sit with Leo for the first time since the twins had attacked him.

Leo poured tea into Alex's cup. "Are you ready to study, or do you need another day to rest, lad?" he said.

But Alex's gaze was abstracted again, he'd gone back into his shell. Leo sighed. "I tell you what, look through this book on Max Planck's work on the quantum world. We can study tomorrow. Promise me you'll read it?" Leo said.

Alex shook his head. He was withdrawn and hadn't spoken to Leo since the twins' near-lethal attack on him, often refusing to eat. The doorbell chimed unexpectedly, and they looked at each other, Alex's eyes wide with fear.

"Go to your room, lad. Let the housemaid see who it is," Leo said, turning down his mouth at yet another confirmation that the boy was terrified of other people after his ordeal. His eyes were sad as Alex disappeared up the stairs to his bedroom.

Leo stood up when he saw Willow following his housemaid into the room. "My lady, what a pleasant surprise. How nice to see you," he said.

"Good day, professor," Willow said, as Leo gestured to the housemaid to leave the room.

Willow walked on the balls of her feet to avoid her high heels damaging the intricate Persian carpet and lifted the skirt of her pink satin dress to sit down next to him on the dark green kissing couch. She pointed her knees towards him and crossed her ankles. The smell of her rose perfume spread softly in the air.

Leo glanced at the housemaid as she retreated, the door clicking shut behind her. "I wasn't expecting you today, my lady," Leo said.

Willow's periwinkle eyes gazed into his heavy-lidded brown ones. "You can start by telling me where that Greek boy from Cyprus has disappeared to, Leo," she said.

Leo's eyes widened. "What makes you think I know where he is?" he said.

Willow caught his disingenuous tone and drew in a frustrated breath. "You know him best, Leo. You see him every day. Don't look so innocent, I know you better than that. Where would he have run off to? The boy has no money or family in England."

Leo needed to buy some time. "May I ask why you want to know?" he said.

Willow crossed her arms. "My children told me he stole some money from the house and ran off with it," she said. "I'm about to call the police on the little thief. When I think about how well we fed him and even gave him a room to stay in while he studied, I can't understand it."

She stood up and took a few steps away from Leo, who looked at her tensed shoulders and sighed. "Willow, do you hear yourself? Do you honestly believe that Alex stole money from you?" he said. "What would he do with it? He barely speaks to anyone; he seems incapable of stealing and is much too shy to take such risks. I know my student."

Willow sat back down next to him and moved closer, plucking at the material of her dress. "I..I... don't know what to believe," she said.

Leo covered her hands with his and put his arm around her shoulder. "I miss you," he murmured.

Willow broke down, bending her head and crying, the light pink satin on her lap darkening with tears. "I miss you too. I can't bear it without you. I'm sorry I accused Alex of stealing," she said. "He doesn't seem capable of it. He was always sweet and shy with me, but why would the twins say that he'd stolen from us?"

Leo wrapped his arms around her. "Tell me why you're so upset," he said.

Willow wiped her tears with a handkerchief. "My children are wicked," she said. "They make my life a misery. I don't know where I went wrong. How did they become so cruel? They say terrible things to me when James's away. And he's right. They're lazy. Oliver sleeps all day. God knows what he gets up to at night."

Willow embraced Leo, pressing his face to hers, lips lingering on his in a long kiss. When it ended, he gently took her arms and put them by her side with an intense look in his eyes. "Listen carefully. I'm sorry to stop you, but this is going to hurt," he said.

Willow tensed up and gripped his hand.

"Regina and Oliver tried to drown the boy in your pond," Leo said. "They almost succeeded. I found him and brought him here. He was barely dressed and had no money or anything else on him, Willow, they nearly killed him."

Willow looked appalled. "Why on earth would they do something like that to a perfect stranger. He was a guest in our home," she said.

Leo's eyes were gloomy. "I don't know, Willow. The attack was entirely unprovoked. Alex wouldn't hurt a fly. He's completely harmless," he said. "Regina and Oliver are bullies of the cruellest kind. We both know that James won't believe Alex against his own children and he could go to prison."

Willow sighed. "You're right, Leo. James might not think much of his children. But he'd do everything in his power to defend them and his family name," she said.

Leo stroked her shoulder. "I have a plan," he said.

"What is it, darling? I'll help in any way I can without betraying my children, beasts though they are. Where is Alex?"

"Never mind the plan, and never mind where he is. It's best if you don't know," Leo said.

She tilted her head, baring her neck. "Alright, Leo, whatever you say, I trust you'll do what's best."

He kissed her collarbone and felt her shoulder relaxing under his lips. "Send your children back to university tomorrow," he said.

Willow's hands clenched into fists. "But they have another three days of holiday. They'll raise hell," she said.

"Don't take no for an answer, tell them that their father insists on it. By the time James returns, I'll have sorted everything out," Leo said.

"James won't be in Cyprus for long," Willow said. "That's why I didn't go with him this time."

Leo's voice was gruff. "It's best if we don't see each other until this all blows over," he said.

The pink satin dress darkened with Willow's tears again. "Leo, our relationship has been a secret for far too long. We must think about our future together. Regina and Oliver are old enough to take care of themselves," she said.

"We'd have to tell James you want a divorce, it's going to be difficult on everyone," Leo said.

Willow played with her locket. "It's the right time. I found out he's been having an affair. He hasn't been in love with me for a long time. He's barely civil because he wants to be with her," she said.

"I see. It might go easier if he wants a divorce too," Leo said.

Willow gathered her coat and bag, then kissed and embraced Leo. "I don't know how long I can carry on living with James. Our marriage has been dead for a long time now," she said on her way out.

Leo watched her walk away and a grimace of regret passed over his face. "Willow!" he called out to her.

She turned back to him.

"I'll find a way for us to be together permanently. I promise, no more sneaking around. I just didn't want to risk your financial security, and divorce can be hard on the children. You know I love you," he said.

"I love you too, Leo. Don't worry about our financial security, we can make do. I don't care about the money. I just want to be with you," Willow said.

Alex watched them embrace from the window overlooking the professor's garden and made a secret symbolic sign with his interlocked fingers. "Shh, shh. Stay together," Alex said under his breath before turning away from the window and going to his bed to lie down again. His lips trembled and he curled into the foetal position for comfort. Tears dripped onto the pillow as he cried silently.

After the twins' attempted murder, Alex had withdrawn even more than usual, crying and screaming internally. His fury against the injustice was a raw pain burning in his stomach and he cried until his throat hurt and his lungs had no more air left in them, leaving him weak and helpless. If it weren't for the ball of light protecting his heart, Alex wouldn't have had a single reason to go on living.

Leo walked into Alex's room to check on him after Willow had left and his heart went out to the young boy who was in so much pain. "Try not to worry. You're safe here," he said.

But Alex refused to speak to Leo and just stared at him mutely through tear-filled eyes. Leo was worried that the damage to his mind was permanent because whenever he brought him a maths problem to solve, Alex would simply look at it, then turn away. He'd go for hours without eating and Leo began to be afraid that he'd starve himself to death.

All Alex wanted to do was walk, and every couple of hours, he'd leave the house, walking for ages before coming back to sit silently in his room. During the long walks, he communed with his spirit guide, Hzartanek. "I don't want to live in this dimension," Alex mind spoke.

"Be patient, the One is with you. You need to stay in this space-time. In this body singularity. We are always here with you," Hzartanek mind whispered.

After communing with the One, Alex would sleep peacefully, knowing his higher power protected him, but still refusing to talk to anyone else. Finally, Leo reached his limit and decided to bring in an expert in psychology.

The day after Willow's visit, the doorbell chimed, and Leo walked into Alex's room with a stranger. "Alexandros, this is Dr Perry Simons. He's a psychiatrist and is here to help you. Talk to him about what's on your mind," Leo said, leaving them alone.

Alex had just woken up and squinted at Dr Simons. The psychiatrist peered back at him through short-sighted eyes. A dark pond appeared out of thin air, hanging suspended between them. Alex's eyes teared up as he and the stunned doctor watched the Merin twins' murder attempt on Alex play out in the mirage.

The image of the pond changed into the opening of a cave ringed by British soldiers. They were training their guns on someone just inside the darkness. Dr Simons couldn't see who it was. The scene changed again, and they watched as a young man surrounded by soldiers was about to be hanged in a prison. After one last look at the doctor, Alex closed his eyes and fell asleep, curled up tight like a baby.

The visions faded from view, leaving Dr Simons struggling to take a breath. He gasped Leo's name as the professor rushed up the stairs, shocked at the sight of the doctor running his hands repeatedly down his green waistcoat as he huffed and puffed.

"What's wrong? You look like you've seen a ghost," Leo said.

Simons was heavyset and his waistcoat strained with each laboured breath. "Yes, I mean, no, nothing happened," he said. "Your ward won't talk to me. He has severe emotional damage. Maybe even brain damage. Did something happen to him?"

Leo avoided answering the question. What if he told Dr. Simons about the twins' attempted murder and he went to the police? "He refused to talk to you, is that what happened? He hasn't said a word to me for a week and I'm the closest thing he has to a friend. Why are you so upset?" Leo said.

"He didn't say anything, at least not verbally. He flinched if I even tried to talk to him," Dr Simons said, avoiding Leo's eyes.

"How do I handle this situation, doctor? What do you recommend?"

Dr Simons sighed as he took his glasses off, then put them back on again. "He could be a schizophrenic but I'm not 100% sure," Dr. Simons said. "He'll need hospitalisation if he gets worse. The boy needs a safe environment. There are some new medicines I could prescribe, but only after more examinations."

"Doctor, I'm in a difficult situation. Alex is a mathematical genius and the government believes he has huge potential. We brought him from Cyprus to study," Leo said.

Dr Simons' expression was adamant. "Absolutely not. I'm afraid that's out of the question in his current condition.

Something's traumatised him, pushed him far away from reality."

Leo rubbed the back of his neck, looking downcast. "I could contact his family in Cyprus. Perhaps he'll feel safer there," he said.

"Yes, that might work. His condition could improve if he goes home. A familiar environment can work wonders," Dr Simons said.

"Thank you for coming," Leo said.

Dr Simons tugged once more at his belaboured waistcoat, muttered 'goodbye' and rushed out of the house, slamming the door behind him. Leo went upstairs, still wondering why he'd been so agitated. He gently shook Alex's shoulders to wake him up. "Alex, you're going back home to Cyprus. Would that make you happy?" Leo said.

Alex's nut-brown eyes brightened at Leo's words. Although he didn't crack a smile, his face lightened with relief and his change of mood was contagious. Leo smiled at his ward. "It'll be alright, lad, you'll see. There's nothing like your home country to make you feel better."

A few days later, Alex and Leo walked up the ship's ramp for his trip back to Cyprus. The sea breeze blew darts of freezing air onto their flinching skin as if their coats didn't exist. At the top of the ramp, Leo turned to Alex and grasped his shoulders. "I'll leave you here. Your teacher, Mr. Georgiades, will pick you up at Limassol Port. You'll stay with him until you feel better. We'll talk by phone. Try to study, everything will be alright," he said.

For once, Alex wasn't afraid of being touched and tolerated Leo's hand on his shoulder, even managing a small smile. "Thank you for everything, professor," he said.

Leo's eyes teared up at Alex's first words since the Merin twins had attacked him. "Goodbye. Remember to study, it'll help you forget what happened," he said.

"I don't need to study. It's all known to me now," Alex said.

"What on earth do you mean?"

Alex gripped Leo's elbow. "I'll see you in Cyprus," he said.

Leo smiled and shook his head. "My dear boy, I live in England. I don't have any plans to visit your island. But if I ever go back there, I'll certainly look you up."

Alex gave him a knowing look and a blinding smile, then turned and boarded the ship without saying goodbye.

As he walked back down the ramp, Leo thought about the telephone conversation he'd had with Alex's father, who had rejected the idea of Alex coming back home to live with him. "I don't want him back. We made a deal that he would stay in England. The Englishman Merin is paying good money for him," Nikos had said.

"But the doctor said he needs a safe place for a while. He's had a nervous breakdown. Don't you have any feelings for his predicament?" Leo said.

Nikos scoffed. "Don't blame me. That boy was never right in the head. It's his mother's fault," he said. "Her whole family is crazy. Anyway, Cyprus isn't safe. Don't you watch the news? He should stay in England. There's a fight against the English here. He's no good to me if he can't work or bring in any money, I don't want him here."

Leo struggled for words. "But - he's your son. He's underage, so you're legally responsible for his wellbeing," he said.

Just before he slammed the phone down, Nikos said, "I told you, are you deaf? He's no son of mine anymore."

On the train home to Oxford, Leo prayed for Alex's safety. He couldn't stop thinking about the boy's fate. "The poor lad," he said to himself as the plush green English countryside flashed by the train window. It started raining, echoing his mood and Leo felt the urge to find Willow at all costs. If he could talk to her about Alex, perhaps they could find a solution together. Alex would be an orphan even though his parents were alive, so someone had to care for him in his vulnerable state.

Chapter 5

It was a warm day when the ship arrived at Limassol Port and Mr Georgiades was waiting as Alex walked down the ramp. The Mediterranean Sea glittered behind the ship, a shimmering expanse of breath-taking shades of cyan and ultramarine blues.

"You've lost weight, Alex. My wife has prepared your favourite foods to put some meat on your bones," Mr. Georgiades said, clucking his tongue.

On the way to the car, Alex stared at the line of British soldiers guarding the port with blank, unsettling expressions.

"Things have been bad, Alex," Mr. Georgiades said. "Fighting, violence, terrible times. We don't know what will happen next. EOKA and the British are on the verge of all-out war. Whatever happens, we must still carry on with our studies."

Mr. Georgiades chattered during the drive back to Nicosia, hardly noticing Alex's complete silence. The boy ignored his teacher and stared out of the window, taking in the green fields and perfect blue sky over the brown-grey foothills around Limassol. A slight smile touched Alex's lips; this was his favourite season. The soft spring light played on yellowish-green fields and danced on the red poppies and orange wildflowers scattered around the countryside. The air was clear that spring. It had a sweet, soft glow, unlike the summertime when the sun's glare reflected off every surface like a spotlight.

Alex mind spoke with Hzartanek. "My country's in trouble."

"We sense that as far as the 17th dimension. Dangerous imbalances have developed," Hzartanek mind spoke.

"What should I do?"

"Keep up your walking quests. We work through you. The One will restore the multi-versal balance," came the answer.

As soon as they reached Mr. Georgiades' home in Nicosia old town, Alex went on a walking quest around the familiar, narrow streets. The quiet felt dangerous and a sharp smell of gunpowder contrasted with the sweet smell of jasmine. Alex was further unnerved when patrolling British soldiers gave him hard looks. One of them walked towards him and stopped when Alex flinched away.

On his way back to the house on Ermou Street, Alex heard someone following him and looked over his shoulder. A few of the British soldiers were behind him. He sped up to a run for the last few feet and dashed into the small concrete yard. The soldiers picked up the pace and clattered through the gate on his heels. One of them grabbed Alex by the shoulder. He had a missing front tooth and a stocky body with hard, calloused hands. Alex's mouth gaped open in shock. He touched his heart with his left hand to call on Hzartanek.

Mr Georgiades burst out of the house. "What are you doing here? Leave him alone. He's just a boy!" he shouted.

"We caught him breaking the curfew! When will you stupid Cypos learn to follow the rules?" the soldier shouted back, drawing his gun, mouth twisted with hatred. The soldier bared his teeth and Alex stared down the barrel of a gun pointed at his head.

"No, no, wait a minute, there's no need..." Mr. Georgiades said, making a soothing motion with his palms.

They all turned as the gate squeaked and opened behind them. Sir James walked into the small yard, sharp eyes taking in the scene. He struck his walking stick on the ground with a crack. "What are you doing, private? Put that gun away now!" he said. The authority in his voice was compelling.

"Yes, sir!" said the soldier, lowering his gun and his eyes and standing to rigid attention.

Sir James said: "Get out of here, all of you. I expect you'll be hearing from your sergeant about your lack of discipline, and it won't be pleasant. Now, move!"

The soldiers shuffled out of the yard. Sir James stared at Alex, who was hugging himself and moaning in fear. "Don't worry, lad. They won't harm you now," he said. "Willow told me you'd disappeared. I don't know why you're here instead of in Oxford, but I intend to find out. Meanwhile, stay put for your own safety."

Mr. Georgiades looked up at Sir James. "Thank you, sir, you saved the boy's life. It's a miracle you were nearby."

Sir James snorted. "It's no miracle. I'm here because Leo Carter asked me to talk with you and it was on my way to inspect the troops." he said. "Please take care of the lad for the time being. The political situation here is getting worse. You should find a safe place. Take some money to help with food."

Mr. Georgiades took the money and gave the governor a grateful look. "Thank you, that's very kind of you, sir."

The tutor took Alex into the kitchen for a hot cup of tea sweetened with condensed milk. "There, there now. This will calm your nerves. It was lucky Sir James stepped in to save your life," he said to the still shaking boy. "He appears quite fond of you. God knows what's going to happen next, but it helps that someone so powerful is protecting you."

But Alex refused to calm down and kept looking over his shoulder in case the governor came back – this time with his children.

April 1955

It was the 1st of April, and a loud 'bang' woke Alex up from a night of light sleep. The house shook in the explosion, and he tumbled out of bed as a siren started howling from somewhere too close for comfort. Mr. Georgiades and his wife rushed into his room.

"Alex, come with us. We've got to hide in the basement. EOKA has attacked the British army. It's war!" Mr. Georgiades said, waving his arms. As Alex hesitated, Mr. Georgiades picked the boy up and threw him over his shoulder. "There's no time for this," he said.

As they reached the basement door, Mr. Georgiades lowered Alex to the floor. Alex touched his heart to call on Hzartanek's protection, then turned and ran away, ignoring his foster parents' desperate shouts. "Hzartanek, what should I do? The war we feared has started," Alex mind spoke.

"Start a walking quest now. Just walk. The One will protect you. We are channelling through you to restore balance," Hzartanek mind spoke.

Alex slowed his pace, focused on the road and walked. Halfway up Xanthis Xenierou Street, he passed the same British patrol that had attacked him the day before. They glared at him as he walked past them. "Think you've got yourself a big protector, boy? Better watch your back. He won't be here forever," shouted the soldier who'd held a gun to his head.

Alex glided past the group of soldiers without even looking at them, the walking quest taking all his attention. The private turned away and grumbled under his breath as he remembered the sergeant's harsh discipline of the night before.

Hzartanek walked side-by-side with Alex, whispering calculations and probabilities into his mind. "Go left here, step on that stone, sit on this bench," it mind spoke.

Alex rubbed his bald head. "How does this help?" he mind-spoke.

"Your walks amplify and spread our power around you. We work through your mind and body to radiate peaceful waves of balance and harmony in the surrounding space," Hzartanek mind spoke.

"But does anyone care? All I see is hatred and hostility. How can energy waves help?" Alex mind spoke.

"Waves turn to particles. Particles become thoughts. Thoughts transform into actions. Cross that road. Step on the crack. Go up those stairs," Hzartanek mind spoke.

The list of whispered instructions was incessant, taking Alex step-by-step through the warren of faded roads lined with the facades of deeply recessed sandstone houses. Alex and Hzartanek floated through the narrow streets, many with pavements just half a meter wide. The interiors of the houses were deceptively spacious and all that Alex could see from the road were high shutters and balconies with ornately curved ironwork. On the way back home, the roads were empty and silent and a faint luminescence floated behind Alex. Mr. Georgiades' face was pale and pinched when he walked into the house. "Never do that again, Alexandros. Someone might have killed you. What's it like out there?" he said.

Alex made a strange sign with his hands, holding his palms a few inches away from each other as if cupping a bowl. Then he just curled up into a ball and went to sleep while the adults looked at each other and sighed. Mrs. Georgiades clucked her tongue. "God bless him. His guardian angel is working overtime," she said.

In the following days of the war of independence between EOKA and the British army, Alex went on one walking quest after another, protected by his weird luck. By then, he was just 15 years old.

1960

Five years after the war of independence against British rule, Cyprus' future looked brighter. After the peace agreement, Britain and Cyprus struck up an alliance and all the while, Alex went on daily walking quests with Hzartanek guiding him each step of the way. On June 1st, Alex came back from a walk and opened the front door to Mr. Georgiades' home where he'd been living ever since his father refused to take him back in 1955. As he walked in, Mrs. Georgiades' scream jabbed at his sensitive ears and he ran into the living room to see his teacher lying on the floor, unconscious.

The ambulance crew looked sombre as they carried the stretcher to the waiting vehicle and Mrs. Georgiades went with them in the ambulance. After they'd left, Alex waited motionless in the kitchen until Mrs Georgiades came back several hours later, sobbing. "My dear Alexandros, your teacher is dead, he had a heart attack," she said in a trembling voice, holding her husband's suit jacket to her chest.

Alex shook his head, he could clearly see a vision of his teacher standing in the middle of the room, holding out a ham sandwich with his kind smile reassuring him one last time. "Don't cry, auntie. My teacher is still here with you. I can see him now," Alex said.

Mrs Georgiades looked at Alex through uncomprehending, tear-filled eyes. He spoke so rarely that his sudden fluency took her by surprise. She scanned the empty room twice over and wept again. "What will become of you, Alexandros? I can't take care of you on my own."

Chapter 6

Violet storm clouds scudded across the sky over Oxford, shadowing the gentle English sun as Leo walked towards the Merin's mansion and rang the doorbell. Willow opened the door and in answer to her worried look, he took her fine-boned hands in his and kissed her lightly on the cheek. "It's time. Everything will be alright, trust me," he said.

Holding hands, they walked together into the study where Sir James was sitting at his desk. He looked at their clasped hands and stood up. "Leo?" he said.

Leo let go of Willow's hand and walked towards James. "Willow and I are in love," he said.

James held his gaze for a moment, then sat down, crestfallen. "How long has this been going on?" he said.

"Ten years, James. I'm sorry to hurt you. I wanted to protect the children and give them a chance to grow up before we did anything about our relationship," Willow said.

James looked at her, reddened eyes glazed over as tears threatened. "I'm not surprised. I haven't treated you well, Willow," he said, bracing his shoulders. "I'm in love with someone else and have been for some time. I didn't know how to tell you."

Willow's eyes filled with empathy for her powerful, distant husband. "I've known about her for a long time, James, I even know her name. I'm happy for you, I want you to know that."

She touched James's hand. "I want a divorce."

James withdrew his hand. "I want a divorce too, Willow. You don't have to worry about money. I'll provide for your needs. The lawyer will handle it," he said.

They turned at the sound of the study door slamming, and saw that Oliver had walked in as they were talking. "Father, she just told you she's been cheating on you for 10 years. How can you forgive her when she's acting like a streetwalker?" he shouted.

James strode over to Oliver and cuffed him around the ear. "Don't talk about your mother like that, have some respect!" he said.

Oliver's eyes filled with tears and his face reddened as he threw himself at his father. "I hate you! Why do you love everyone else but me?" he yelled.

In the next instant, James had restrained Oliver and pushed him out of the study door. "You're drunk. Control yourself and go to your room, I don't want to hear any more of your nonsense," he said in a clipped tone.

Leo took a deep breath and gripped Sir James's shoulder. "I'm sorry it's come to this, please believe me that we didn't want to harm anyone in the family," he said.

Sir James shrugged his hand off and turned away. "Just go now, Leo, and take Willow with you," he said.

Regina stood by the study door with her arms crossed, glaring daggers as Willow and Leo walked past her. She opened her mouth to speak but the sound of shattering glass interrupted her. They heard a short scream and a heavy thump outside the house. Regina was the first to run into the garden, Willow on her heels. Oliver was lying on the grass, his head at a strange angle.

"No!" Willow screamed.

"You killed him," Regina said in a calm voice, face expressionless. "You'll regret this."

Willow's legs gave way and she collapsed to the ground. Leo kneeled beside her and held her as she sobbed. Sir James walked slowly to Oliver's body and picked him up, turning to Leo and Willow with his son in his arms.

"Leo, leave now and don't come back," he said, lips working.

Willow leaned on Leo as they walked down the driveway and he put his arms around her shoulders and waist as her legs buckled. "We'll talk to them when things calm down," Leo said as Willow sobbed on the short walk home.

A few days later, Sir James's lawyer, Jonas Smithson, turned up at Leo's house. "As part of the divorce settlement, Sir James has generously offered to buy you a house in Nicosia," Jonas Smithson said in Leo's study.

"In Nicosia? Why? What about the arrangements for Oliver's funeral?" Willow said with a confused look on her face.

"It's a condition of the divorce that you leave England," the lawyer answered. "Sir James insists on it. If you agree, you won't have to worry about money for the rest of your life. Oliver's funeral has already taken place in the family plot. Only Sir James and Regina attended."

Willow turned away, hugging her stomach. "James should have told me. He was my son, too," she said.

"What about my teaching career at Oxford?" Leo said.

The lawyer looked down at his papers. "Sir James has arranged for a new position. You'll be a consultant for a British petroleum company in Cyprus. The pay is triple your current salary," he said, standing up to leave. "You have 48 hours to respond to the terms."

Leo turned to Willow. "What do you…"

The slamming of a door interrupted him, and Regina walked into the room, her icy blue eyes narrowed in spite. "You traitor. Did you leave us for him? That nobody?" she said.

As Willow shrank into herself, Leo stood up and moved between her and Regina. "You have no right to speak to your mother like that. Apologise or leave if you can't be civil," he said.

Regina's laugh was hard and scornful. "I'll never apologise to that thing. She's nothing to me, least of all my mother," she said.

Willow wrapped her arms around her chest. "Regina, darling, please try to understand. I'm sorry if the divorce hurts you," she said.

Regina pushed Leo in the shoulder and he stumbled backwards, jostling Willow. "Hurts me? You're joking. I'm glad you're out of the way. I'll make sure everyone knows you're responsible for Oliver's suicide," she said, slamming the door behind her as she left.

Leo held Willow as she cried. "Mr. Smithson, tell Sir James we agree to the terms. We'll have a fresh start in Cyprus. Send the papers through to me," he said.

Six months later, they'd settled in Nicosia, and it didn't take long for Leo to find Mrs Georgiades and visit her to discuss Alex's future. Alex ran out of his room when he heard Leo's voice, face wreathed in one of his rare, incandescent smiles. "I told you I'd see you here, professor," he said.

The widow wore the traditional black skirt and blouse she would wear for the rest of her life. "Leo, it's good to see you," Mrs. Georgiades said. "This must be the first time Alex has left his room since my husband died. The truth is, I can't take care of him by myself. We don't get along the way he and my husband did when he was alive."

Leo grasped Alex by the shoulder. "Willow and I would be happy to look after him," he said. Alex's smile was all they needed to see, and the couple took him in until they found a place not too far away from their home where he could live on his own.

They soon became familiar with his daily long walks around the imposing headquarters of the Orthodox Church. The palace grounds housed a curved old sandstone church with jewel-like stained glass windows, surrounded by elegant buildings containing courtrooms and archives. Since independence, the palace had become a political power centre and the leader of the church, Archbishop Makarios, was preparing to take over as the country's president.

One baking summer's night, Alex burst breathlessly into the house, motioning frantically for Leo to follow him and they disappeared into the night. Willow, who was pregnant with her third child, Sam, worried at her collarbone with her fingertips as she watched them walk away.

It was hard to breathe in the still, hot air as Alex led Leo to a large tree on the avenue in front of the palace and put his finger in front of his mouth, motioning Leo to be quiet. Leo cocked his head and lifted his palms to say, 'what's happening?' Alex pointed to the entrance close to the archbishop's parked car.

Two armed and masked figures dressed in black crouched on either side of the gates. In the bright moonlight, Leo dimly made out a tattoo of a claw on the arm of one of the masked figures. They shuffled behind the tree as quietly as they could but weren't stealthy enough and Leo stepped on a discarded can which crackled into the silence.

One of the masked intruders whipped around, raising a gun as Leo and Alex ran for cover, hearts pounding, their pursuers' footsteps echoing behind them. They ducked into one of the narrow streets lining the palace area and hid inside a garage, holding their breath as the masked figures strode past their hiding place. One of them yanked off the balaclava and the moonlight shone on a stark black claw tattoo on her arm. Blond hair tumbled and tossed to her shoulders as she raked it away from her face with long fingers. "Jesus. It's hot in this godforsaken country," she said.

Leo's eyes widened as he recognised Regina's voice.

"Let's go back and finish the job. To hell with them, whoever they were. Probably just some neighbourhood kids," Regina hissed.

The man with her pulled off his mask and moved closer to Regina to murmur in her ear. "If we kill Makarios now, we'll get caught. They saw us, so we must be patient and wait for another opportunity," he said.

"Reclamation won't wait, Saunders," Regina spat. "We swore an oath to take control of Cyprus' resources. We know there's money to be made from oil and gold here. Besides, if they report it to the police now, it'll give them a chance to increase security around Makarios."

As he heard his tormentors' voice, Alex trembled uncontrollably in his hiding place, and he repeatedly touched his heart. Leo shot him a reassuring look and put his finger to his mouth.

Regina's head turned as she heard shouts coming from the Archbishop's Palace and guards ran towards them, one of them firing a warning shot in the air. The would-be assassins sprinted around the corner and Leo heard the screech of tyres as they gunned the engine of a high-powered vehicle. The sound of the engine dwindled into the distance as they got away.

Alex and Leo stayed hidden from the guards, fearing they'd be shot by mistake. When it was safe, Leo called the police and went with them to the Archbishop's Palace to warn them about Regina.

After it was all over, Leo and Willow sat at their kitchen table. "What happened tonight? Why was Alex so scared and where did you run off to?" Willow said.

Leo took a long sip of single malt whiskey. "Regina tried to assassinate Archbishop Makarios," he said.

Willow's hand went to her throat. "What do you mean? Regina's here?" she said.

"Yes, in Nicosia, we stopped them just in time. She was with someone, a man. They had black tattoos on their arms," Leo said.

Willow picked up the telephone and called her ex-husband. "I'll ask James. He'll know what's going on with Regina," she said.

"Did you know that Regina is here in Cyprus?" she said when Sir James answered the phone.

"No, I haven't seen her since she got married," came the answer.

Willow heard his cane tapping on the ground. "Who did she marry and why did she do it so quickly?" she said.

Sir James huffed and sighed. "She married Lord Addington. I don't know why. She didn't invite me to the wedding. Wouldn't have gone anyway. We haven't spoken since Oliver, since he... Anyway, I don't know," he said.

Willow took a deep breath. "Addington. Isn't he…"

"Yes, that Addington. Helped sponsor uprisings in several ex-colonies. Mopped up the mining rights during the chaos," Sir James said.

"Something strange is going on. She tried to assassinate Makarios tonight. The police have an arrest warrant out for her," Willow said.

"I'll keep an eye out. Not much more I can do; I've had nothing to do with her ever since that ridiculous court case to claim her and Oliver's trust fund. She told the most monstrous lies."

"Thank you, James. I hope you're...Are you well?"

"Yes, yes, well enough. I remarried too, just a few months now."

Willow paused. "Congratulations, I wish you every happiness," she said.

Chapter 7

1974

Alex spent his days on walking quests through the streets of old Nicosia with Hzartanek whispering instructions each step of the way.

"Stop," Hzartanek mind spoke.

Alex stood stock-still on the street next to the Ay. Savva Church, the eaves sheltering him from a light rain. Above him was an open window in a stately sandstone house. Loud voices floated through the window and echoed off the opposite wall on the narrow street.

"We can't let Cyprus be independent. It's gone far enough," a familiar voice said.

Alex trembled as he recognised Regina's harshly clipped British accent and remembered the terrifying moments when he thought he would drown at her hands.

"We undermine the Republic whenever we can but it's still gaining credibility. It's not in Turkey's interests to have a free Cyprus," a stranger answered in a heavy Turkish accent.

"What about the idea of triggering a civil war between the Greeks and Turks here, Ambassador Esen? You never answered me about Turkey's intentions. Will you help my organisation?" Regina said.

There was a long silence before the Turkish ambassador said: "What is your plan, Lady Addington? How will we do such a thing without the international community sanctioning us?"

"Nobody but you and our backers in the British government knows about Reclamation. No one will expose Turkey as being part of the plot," Regina said.

"Your plan won't work. The British have lost their influence in Cyprus," Ambassador Esen said.

"If you think you don't need us anymore, remember the Cypriot militants are ready to go for the jugular. EOKA B loathes the TMT. A single spark could start a fire," Regina said.

"And if that happens, Turkey could intervene, according to our guarantor rights," Ambassador Esen said.

"Yes, ambassador. Then we can split the island's mining rights," Regina said.

"And what do your British government backers want for this – um - help?" said Ambassador Esen.

The voices faded away and Alex walked back to his small flat on Xanthis Xenierou Street where he ate a ham sandwich in his tiny kitchen, washing it down with a tart, sweet, fresh lemonade he'd bought from a bakery on the way. From the kitchen, Alex took three steps to his bedroom and fell asleep on the narrow bed set against the wall. He always went to sleep at 7:30 pm and was up at 4:00 am for his first walk when Hzartanek woke him up with whispered instructions.

On April 6th, it was drizzling again, as it so often does in spring. Hzartanek told Alex to walk back to the Turkish ambassador's home next to the Ay. Savva Church. A ponderous man with a puffed-out chest and flat feet walked out of the front door with several servants tailing him, bowing and speaking to him in Turkish. As Alex approached the dignitary, Hzartanek mind whispered, "stop, touch your heart."

Alex touched his heart and came to an abrupt stop in front of the official. The Turkish ambassador turned to look at the thin man in shabby clothes standing opposite him, oblivious to the rain. Esen patted down the silky material of his suit and lifted his chin. "Look him in the eyes," Hzartanek mind whispered.

The ambassador backed away, confused by the direct eye contact with the stranger standing so close to him. As he watched, Alex appeared to grow into a giant with stars revolving around his enormous head and shoulders, and Esen shrank back at the illusion, rushing pell-mell into the house. His servants scrambled behind him and one of them waved his arms to shoo Alex away.

Once he'd scurried around the corner, Alex passed a coffee shop with tables set out on the pavement. Traditional red and green woven Cypriot chairs lined the tables and the pungent, cardamom-tinged smell of Cypriot coffee wafted around the street.

"Stop. Sit on the pavement," Hzartanek mind-spoke.

Alex sat with his head hanging between his knees, and could hear a man with a British accent just behind him who was deep in conversation with a Cypriot dressed in black trousers and a white shirt. The Cypriot man clicked and flickered traditional Greek prayer beads in his hands. The beads flashed lapis lazuli blue as they clacked between his fingers.

"Turkish militants are plotting to assassinate the leadership of EOKA B," the British stranger said. "You need to strike before the TMT does or there could be a massacre. My organisation has plenty of money and guns to give you to fight back."

Although they were speaking in low tones, Alex's hearing was so sensitive he could make out every word. He sidled away; fearful they'd spot him, but the men were too involved in their conversation.

"Who are you talking about, Saunders? What are the names of the TMT members and why do they want to attack us?" the Greek-Cypriot man said.

"I have information about a TMT family I suspect of planning an attack. I overheard one of their servants talking," the Saunders said. "They're close relatives of Rauf Denktash and they hate the Greeks. You know the St. Savva Church? That's where they live. Start with them."

"Stand up, walk away," Hzartanek mind whispered.

As Alex left, the customers in the coffee shop didn't even glance at him, he was so adept at avoiding attention.

"How will we stop a full-on civil war? Regina and Saunders are spreading poison. There'll be more conflict between the Greek-and-Turkish Cypriots," Alex mind spoke.

"There's not much chance of balancing this situation. It will help weaken their plot if the Turkish ambassador leaves after his scare," Hzartanek mind whispered.

Alex gritted his teeth. "We can't let Regina win. We must stop them."

Alex went back to the same coffee shop on his next walk, hoping to learn more about the plot. This time, Regina was sitting with Saunders and a third man, a Turkish-Cypriot. Alex recognised him from the news and sat on the pavement near their table. None of them even glanced at the shabby man who was so much part of the street scene he was almost invisible.

"Is the TMT going to sit and do nothing? I told you, EOKA B is planning to attack you. Right at this moment, they're plotting to wipe you all out," Regina said.

"How do you know this information? We've heard nothing. I'm second-in-command of TMT, I'd be the first to know if EOKA B was up to anything," the Turkish-Cypriot man said.

"Don't question me. You know my husband's power. Our agent has confirmed the plot. Tell him, Saunders," Regina said.

"Make Denktash act now or EOKA B will slaughter you all," Saunders said. "Our organisation has money and weapons. We'll help you protect yourselves from the Greeks."

The Turkish-Cypriot man crossed his arms. "Why should I believe you? Do you work with the British government?" he said.

"We can't talk about it. Do you want the guns and money or not?" Regina said, looking over her shoulder to make sure there were no police around.

"He's playing a double game. The Turkish-Cypriot TMT and EOKA B are deadly enemies," Alex mind spoke.

"To kill the island's chances of independence," Hzartanek mind whispered.

"Why is it so important for Cyprus to be independent, Hzartanek?"

"It's at the centre of a universal energy sphere. Cyprus' energetic waves reverberate millions of light-years away from here," Hzartanek mind whispered.

"In another dimension?"

"Yes, in all the dimensions that the sphere occupies. If the quantum field becomes unbalanced by war, it harms the other dimensions of the sphere."

"What do you want me to do?" Alex mind spoke.

"Walk to the market. All rumours gather there on the grapevine. We may hear something useful. Then go to Leo Carter. Tell him what is happening. He will know what to do."

The farmers held their market in a large barn-like building in the old town with plastic containers full of colourful produce. Oranges and lemons were stacked next to bananas and apples. Leafy vegetables like chard, cauliflower and broccoli were lined up with cucumbers and tomatoes and the sharp spicy smell of cracked coriander, olive oil and salt wafted from glass containers full of green olives.

The stallholders had been sipping Zivania since the early morning hours. The high-octane homemade spirit was used to combat the flu and was thought to cleanse bacteria from the intestines, giving them the courage to boast about their prices and wares. They sang and shouted about whatever was on the news, vying for customers. Some of them were over 70 years old with hearing problems, which didn't diminish their enthusiasm or their volume in the least.

The colours captured Alex's attention as he walked around listening to the stallholders' loud conversations about the tensions between the Greek-and-Turkish Cypriot militant groups EOKA B and TMT. Alex listened and learned, then he walked to Leo Carter's place to tell him about Regina's provocative plot. Alex tapped on the door and smiled at Leo when he opened it. As they sat in the Carter's sunlit, airy kitchen, he wolfed down a ham sandwich.

"You were hungry, Alex. Have you been walking again?" Leo said.

"Yes. Regina is plotting to start a civil war between the nationalists," Alex said.

Leo sat down at the table. "How on earth do you know this?" he said.

"I heard them. Hzartanek was with me on the street."

"Who is Hzartanek?"

"He is one and many. He protects me," Alex said.

Leo smiled. "Is he here now?"

"Yes."

"Can you prove it? Show me something," Leo said.

Alex took a breath and listened to the mind whispers. "Hzartanek says you must visit your doctor as your heart needs…" Alex hesitated as he looked for a word. "To flow."

Leo touched his chest. "My heart needs to flow?" he said.

"Yes."

Leo sat back in his chair. "Well, I feel fine. I'll go to Dr. Fellas tomorrow if you insist. Meanwhile, I'll think about how to stop Regina from causing more trouble," he said.

"Can I have another sandwich?"

Leo smiled at Alex. "Yes, of course you can." He treasured the moments when Alex opened up to him and sometimes, he saw flashes of his old brilliance. But so far, Alex had shown no interest in resuming his maths studies, resisting Leo's frequent attempts to interest him in the subject he loved so much. All that Alex would say was that he no longer needed instructions or tutoring because he believed all the laws of physics and maths had been revealed to him, and there was nothing left to learn.

At the appointment with the surgeon, Dr. Fellas listened to Leo's heart through a stethoscope. "I want you to have an electrocardiogram right away," the doctor said, packing his stethoscope back into its case.

"What's wrong with my heart?" Leo said with a worried look.

"It might be nothing. But I prefer to be safe than sorry. You may have a heart murmur," the doctor said.

"But I feel fine."

"Please, just do the test to be safe."

The ECG results showed a blocked heart valve, shocking Leo in more ways than one and proving that Hzartanek's warning had been true.

"It's lucky we caught it now. What made you think to check your heart? It most likely saved your life. Usually these problems are not detected until a heart attack," Dr Fellas said.

Leo looked away. "Just an instinct," he said.

"You must have heart surgery right away. You're still relatively young. After a routine operation, you'll live a long and healthy life," the doctor said.

Leo thanked his lucky stars and thought of Alex, who was on another walking quest in the town centre, where humidity hung in a thin mist near the Saint Savva Church. Alex was close to the Turkish Ambassador's house, and around the corner from the coffee shop where Regina and Saunders had met with the militants.

"Stop," Hzartanek mind whispered.

Alex stopped near a house with a wooden front door painted turquoise with red trimming, set high in the wall with large stone steps leading up to it.

"Walk."

Alex walked towards the coffee shop. "What are we doing here?" he mind spoke.

83

"Spreading peace waves to counteract the warriors' energy," Hzartanek answered as a young woman left the house with the turquoise door and went into the coffee shop.

"Why are you so early, Marinella? I wasn't expecting you until six, sweetheart," her uncle said.

"Yes, it was on impulse, Uncle Takis. I thought you might need help with the chores," Marinella said.

"Thanks, sweetie. Check if there are any customers who need drinks."

Marinella walked around each table, greeting the customers, and taking their orders. At one table, a young man sat alone.

"Can I bring you another coffee?" she said to him.

The young man's brown eyes met her dark blue ones and Marinella's hand went to the back of her neck as she smoothed her hair.

"My name is Ersan. What is yours?" he said.

"Marinella."

"Marinella, if you don't mind me saying, where did you get such beautiful and unusual blue eyes? They look like the sea at twilight."

She blushed. "Thank you. My mother is from France. I got her blue eyes," she said.

"And your father?"

"He's Greek-Cypriot from Nicosia. Where do you come from?"

"A Turkish-Cypriot village near Famagusta. Don't take this the wrong way," Ersan said. "I hope you don't think it is disrespectful, but would you like to meet me for an early dinner? My father has a restaurant 10 minutes away from here. That's why I'm in Nicosia today."

"Yes, I'd like that," Marinella said.

At dinner, the couple talked about their fears for the future.

"I heard the militants are preparing to attack each other," Marinella said.

Ersan looked worried. "I heard the same thing. I feel disaster ahead and I don't know how to stop it because I don't have the power," he said.

Marinella gave him a kind look. "Maybe we can talk to our parents, and they can talk to their connections. Cyprus is a small place. Everyone knows each other," she said.

"It might work. It's worth a try."

After dinner, Ersan walked Marinella back to the house with the turquoise door and red trimming. They held hands as they walked. "I feel like I've known you my whole life," Marinella said.

"I feel the same way. Can I take you out to dinner again?"

"I'm working at the coffee shop tonight. I'm free tomorrow night," she said.

The next night, Ersan told Marinella that he had spoken to his father about the rumoured violence between the militants.

"What did he think?" Marinella said.

"He's worried and he promised to speak to some high-up deputies in Denktash's TMT, but couldn't guarantee anything."

"I asked my father to use his influence with EOKA to calm things down," Marinella said.

Ersan took her hand in his. "Let's hope it's enough."

On July 19th, Ersan looked for Marinella in a panic and found her at her uncle's coffee shop. Ersan took her hands, saying: "Marinella, please come with me. The nationalists are killing each other and war is coming. I heard that the Turkish army is about to invade. We can be together. I want to marry you. Do you trust me enough to come with me?"

Marinella hugged him. "Yes. I'll get my clothes."

On the 20th of July, the wail of air raid sirens woke Alex up from a light sleep and he slid on his trousers which hung loose and baggy from his bony hips as he glanced out of the window. The deserted street called to him, and Alex left the house and walked, as he did every day.

All around him was the rumble of war. Tanks rolled past him on the broader avenues ringing the Venetian Walls. Still, he walked. Nearby OXI roundabout, he heard a woman scream for help and quickened his pace, trotting towards the sound of her voice. Two Turkish soldiers held her by the hair and pushed her down on the ground, laughing. The soldiers turned to face Alex as he approached them and when they were distracted, the woman broke free and ran away.

Cursing in Turkish, the soldiers seized him instead and frog-marched him to a group of Cypriots who huddled next to a building in the cul-de-sac at the end of the road. Twenty crying children, women, and teenagers were in the group of prisoners. A guard stood near them and threatened them with a machine gun.

Everyone's heads turned at the sound of guns firing nearby. A troop of 15 Greek soldiers ran toward the Turkish soldiers and they surged towards each other with homicidal venom, fighting with fists, knives, and guns.

When their captors turned their backs, Alex walked away and motioned the other prisoners to follow him. In the confusion, his group quickly disappeared, seemingly vaporized into thin air as they followed him to safety. Alex led them through the narrow, labyrinthine streets he knew so well, pointing out places where they could hide.

On the first day of the Turkish invasion of Cyprus, Alex walked the streets of old Nicosia until midnight. He helped to hide children and women in places only he knew about from his never-ending walking quests, places that nobody could find without a bulldozer.

Just before midnight, Alex heard a woman screaming and entered a ground floor house where he saw a young woman lying prone on the living room floor. One hand was clenched around a table leg. The other was clamped around her dead husband's arm. They had ripped her dress open to the waist. Blood covered her face and hair. A Turkish soldier pinned down her arms and raped her while the others stood by laughing.

Alex left quietly and found a nearby group of ten National Guard soldiers, beckoning them to follow him to the house. The troops walked inside, and Alex heard more fighting. Four shots split the night air and the woman stopped screaming. Alex saw the Cypriot soldiers escorting her out as they took her to hospital. After they'd left, he went back into the house. In front of him, the Turkish soldiers' dead bodies were on the living room floor. None of them appeared to be over 20 years old. He walked home, exhausted.

Ten days into the war, Alex still walked for most of the day, finding food and bringing it to the families he'd helped to hide in the old city. Under Hzartanek's guidance, he'd hidden around 90 people in obscure basements, spaces underneath courtyards, and in abandoned buildings. The Kurdish owner of a grocery shop helped him with a food supply to keep the refugees alive.

Patrolling Turkish army squads barely gave the bony walking man a second look. If they paid attention to him, it was to mock him for being mentally ill. Alex would play stupid and stare at them with his mouth agape, flinching away from his tormentors so they'd take him for a fool. The soldiers would jeer, then turn around and ignore him.

As the Turkish army advanced, much of the fighting was in north Nicosia. Alex rescued and hid refugees as far from the military camps as he could, remembering each of their hideouts with pinpoint accuracy. One day, on his way to a refugee hiding place, he spotted a motionless body near a Turkish military camp. A wounded Greek-Cypriot soldier lay in the rubble of a bombed-out building. Alex crept up next to him, careful to stay hidden and touched the soldier's face. It was his old nemesis, Christos.

The bullet had hit his lungs and he was barely alive. His body seemed shrunken, like it was already becoming part of the earth beneath him. Christos's eyes opened and Alex smiled at him reassuringly, touching his heart. The soldier reached slowly into his pocket and pulled out his wallet, giving it to Alex.

"I'm scared, Alexandros. Do you forgive me?"

"Yes. Be at peace," Alex said.

Christos closed his eyes for the last time.

"I'll make sure your mother gets your wallet," whispered Alex as his tears fell onto the Christos' face. For a moment, the noise of war fell silent as the soldier's spirit left the earthly plane.

After a long day of walking quests, Alex took the last batch of food to a family of two. He'd hidden a little girl called Elli and her pregnant mother, Sophie, in a safe place. Elli loved Alex and hugged him with all her six-year-old might every time he slipped into the dank, dark space hidden beneath the old courtyard near Solomou Square. The hiding place was a stone's throw away from the medieval sandstone walls.

Sophie smiled at him, and he ducked his head, placing the bread and cheese on a chair. Alex hunched his shoulders and blushed. "The war will be over soon," he said.

"Can you speak a little louder? I can't hear you," said Sophie.

"The war will be over soon. A few more days, that's all, and you can come out of hiding," Alex said in a louder voice.

Elli squealed. "Yay, we're going home!"

"Elli, be quiet. There might be Turkish soldiers around! Thank you for taking care of us," Sophie whispered.

Alex nodded.

"How do you know the war will end?"

"I just know. I heard it," he said.

By now, Alex had learned to use his words instead of conjuring up illusions to explain his thoughts. Words didn't attract attention.

Hzartanek kept him informed with mind-whispers. He took the information from the field of space, atoms, and quantum dimensions all around. Past, present, it didn't matter to Hzartanek, an infinite being who pulled information from any dimension or point in time and space.

"I hope you're right. I haven't heard anything about my husband. The last I saw of him was three weeks ago when he left to fight the Turks," Sophie said, looking down at her protruding belly to hide her tears from Alex. Elli hugged her crying mother.

"Do you have a photograph of your husband?" he said.

"No, I ran out of the house with nothing except Elli and the clothes on my back. Later, I saw I was holding my diary as well, but I forgot my handbag," Sophie said. "The Turkish soldiers went from door to door in Lefkoniko. We walked and hid for a day and a half before we reached Nicosia." Sophie's hand went to her chest and she took shallow breaths as she pulled at the collar of her dress. Elli cried along with her mother.

"My friends, neighbours, I don't know what happened to them. The Turks shot some of them. The others ran away," Sophie said.

Alex touched his heart. "Hzartanek, I need words," he mind spoke as he took a deep breath.

"Speak, they will flow," Hzartanek mind whispered.

"Lefkoniko is deep in enemy territory now and the Turks have taken over the north. The best hope is that your husband is somewhere on our side of the island," Alex blurted out.

As the words flowed out of his mouth, Sophie and Elli stopped crying and looked at him with wide, tear-filled eyes. They were surprised he'd said over three or four words at the same time because his everyday speech was halting and hesitant. Now it was flowing out of him like a river.

"The Turkish army killed many of us, no matter if they were Greek or Turkish Cypriots," Alex said. "They drove them out of their homes in the north, but our army put up a good fight, considering its size. We must wait a few more days. I know that greater powers are working to stop the war."

"So, we can't go home. What will we do?" Sophie said.

"When they put the guns away, we can look for your relatives and friends from Lefkoniko. Hopefully, most of them are on our side by now," Alex said.

Sophie cried again and set Elli off at the same time.

"Eat your food. I'll be back tomorrow with more news," Alex said, as he hurried out of their hiding place.

Sophie and Elli's emotions overwhelmed Alex, who couldn't handle the intensity of his empathy for the mother and daughter. The war had worn on his nerves, but Hzartanek gave him the strength to keep walking. The next day, Alex found two loaves of bread for the pregnant Sophie and walked in the shadows cast by the massive Venetian Walls on the way to Solomou Square. After making sure that nobody was watching him, Alex slipped into the hiding place to see Sophie and Elli's pale faces glimmering in the semi-darkness.

"Did you see the dogs?" Sophie said.

"What dogs? I didn't see any nearby."

"There was a pack of dogs here 10 minutes ago," Sophie said. "They had a disease. Their skin looked like week-old bread, full of patchy mould. I scared them off, but they almost attacked Elli."

"Keep the trapdoor shut," Alex said.

"I only opened it to get some air. It's so stuffy in here."

"The next time, it could be soldiers instead of dogs. The fighting is still heavy out there," Alex said.

Sophie's eyes were hopeful. "Do you have any news?" she asked.

"Yes. They're talking about a truce," he replied.

"Thank God."

"It's still not safe. Stay here for a few more days."

"I don't know how long my baby will wait to be born."

Alex stepped back suddenly; his eyes wide in alarm.

"Don't worry, it's still early. I'm only seven months along," Sophie said, chuckling at his concern.

Elli skipped around her mother. "There's a baby in your belly," she sang.

Sophie held her hands and turned around with her in the cramped space: "Whisper, baby girl, whisper. Remember what we said?"

"Okay, mama," whispered Elli.

"Stay awhile, Alex. We get lonely down here," Sophie said.

"I can't. There are others. I must take them food and clean water," Alex said.

"It's so good of you to take care of us. You're our hero, Alex. We wouldn't have survived without you."

"It's not just me. I have friends. My friend Hzartanek helps me," Alex said as he left the hiding place.

Several days later, the fighting stopped when the sides agreed on a truce after heavy international pressure on Turkey to halt its brutal invasion of tiny Cyprus. Alex took Sophie and Elli to the General Hospital close to Solomou Square. Crying refugees jostled each other on the road and others were beyond tears, staring at the ground as they trudged toward the hospital.

The corridors in the L-shaped Nicosia General Hospital were full of patients waiting to have cholera vaccines. A cholera epidemic had broken out after the month-long war destroyed the island's infrastructure and contaminated the water supply. Elli pointed at a pack of dogs lurking near the entrance to the hospital. The dogs were lank and when they bared their fangs, foamy saliva dripped from their mouths to the dusty ground.

"Look, mama, doggies."

"Don't go near them, Elli. They look sick," Sophie said.

A passing doctor overheard their conversation. "Stay well clear of them," he said. "The dogs eat raw meat and have contagious intestinal diseases. They'll all have to be rounded up and put to sleep to prevent more diseases from spreading."

The maternity ward was relatively empty, and Sophie was lucky enough to get a bed for the night in case her contractions started. There was nowhere else for her to go until they could locate her relatives, so Alex made sure she was comfortable and left after she and Elli had fallen asleep. A week later, he returned to visit Sophie, who smiled at him over a baby in a blue blanket.

"Congratulations, he came early," Alex said.

"Not he - she - they only had blue blankets. I called her Marina," Sophie said.

"She's my baby sister," Elli announced from her chair next to Sophie.

"Is there any news about your husband?" Alex said.

"Not yet. I found my uncle through the nurses here," Sophie said. "The doctors treated him for a gunshot wound, and they sent him a message to meet me when he feels better. My uncle will help us to find my husband."

Elli ran to hug his knees with all her six-year-old might and a rare smile lit up Alex's gaunt face.

Back in his tiny kitchen on Xanthis Xenierou Street, Alex stared at the ham sandwich he'd made earlier. He laid his head on his arms and fell asleep at the table, waking up at 4:00 am without his usual strength to walk, not even when Hzartanek asked him to. Hours turned into days and what little food he had went stale but he couldn't force himself to leave his tiny flat to find rations. Alex grew even thinner and slept for most of the day, hugging his knees to his chest.

On the fourth day, just before he saw nothing more, Elli's smile flashed through his mind. Leo found him several days later and took him in where he recovered from exhaustion with Willow and Sam, who had grown into a bright teenager and shared Alex's passion for maths and physics.

The Green Line, 1975

Regina faced down the Greek-Cypriot policeman who had confronted her next to the buffer zone in Nicosia. He'd recognised her from the arrest warrant and shouted at her to stop. Regina sneered at the lone cop, venom shining from her ice-blue eyes.

Like shadows, four Turkish soldiers appeared from a bombed-out shell of a building where they'd been hiding near the Green Line. They levelled their guns at the policeman, who went white with fear and staggered back a few steps.

Regina turned and fled across the truce line to north Cyprus, protected by the Turkish soldiers. Her husband was fuming when she told him of her confrontation with the Greek-Cypriot policeman. "Don't cross the truce line until I give the word, it's too hot at the moment," Lord Addington said.

"But the Turks haven't finished the job," Regina said.

"The world's turned against Turkey, we have to be careful and lay low for a while."

Regina stared out of the window of her mansion overlooking Kyrenia Bay. "I don't care how long it takes," she said. "Reclamation is only a matter of time."

Part II

Chapter 8

Xanthis Xenierou Street, 2010

The gaunt old man was an enigma.

Even before Rebecca Vassiliou looked up from her computer, she sensed that the movement she'd caught on the road was her neighbour. As he passed her window, she looked straight into the old man's eyes. A wave of vertigo flooded through her, and her vision felt sucked into a vortex that appeared between them. Their gazes locked and it felt like the rest of the world had been suspended outside the tunnel vision between them.

The old man broke the spell when he averted his eyes, hitched his trousers up over bony hips and walked past her window. Drivers honked their horns, urging him to move out of the middle of the road, but the discordant clamour fell on deaf ears. The old man didn't change his gait or pace until he'd disappeared up the stairs leading to the parallel road.

Rebecca let out a breath she hadn't realised she'd been holding and shook her head, chiding her over-active imagination. She'd been working too hard, or maybe the heat was getting to her. Even in the hottest weather, her neighbour walked up the road to Eleftheria Square holding a plastic bag with a sandwich he'd bought on a street corner. She'd never seen him without a cigarette hanging loosely between his lips with his jaw jutted out to keep it in place.

The walker's worn and dirty shirt was a dusty grey the sun couldn't brighten, no matter how hard it shone. His trousers were thin and tattered around his ankles, and their bottoms barely brushed against his cracked shoes. A belt that had seen better days kept his trousers from dropping over his protruding hip bones.

He'd walked the same route ever since she could remember and seemed to be an integral part of the neighbourhood, like the faded paint on the doors of the closely packed houses, or the smell of heated tarmac on the road. Despite his frailty, he endured, reminding her of the crumbling medieval sandstone walls that formed a protective ring around the heart of the old town.

Rebecca had been a child when she'd first spotted the old man. She'd lived with her English father and Greek-Cypriot mother in the same area twenty years ago. The sight of him brought back the old pain of losing them but she didn't resent the reminder, though. Seeing him walk by brought back memories of her childhood years when she was lucky enough to have them in her life.

Rebecca's eyes misted over with wistful memories. *"Mummy, why does the old man walk all day,"* she would ask.

"Quiet, mouse, don't be rude, he might not like being called old. Look how lightly he walks, like a young man. Be a good girl now," her mother would say, stroking Rebecca's soft blond hair with

hands that smelled of cigarettes, fresh nail polish and Ponds cream. From then on, Rebecca nicknamed him light walker.

Her parents would take her for walks along the Venetian Walls that ringed the old city, lifting her up and swinging her along as they followed the sandstone walls leading to the 11 heart-shaped bastions. Rebecca would run her hands across the rough pores of the sandstone walls, which were hard but flaked easily under her fingernails.

Decades later, the massive, arched gates opened out to an ever-growing modern city. Ensuing generations of town planners had to design radiating circles around old Nicosia to accommodate the growing population and the whooshing, honking stream of traffic travelling in and out of the city centre.

Rebecca's gaze drifted to the other people walking down the street. Restless migrants and refugees who had made Nicosia their home moved up and down the road, adding layers of character with pasts of their own.

Watching the light walker brought more of her own life back in snatches of memory. He'd walked through her childhood, her psychology studies abroad and her return to Cyprus to start her career. Rebecca shifted in her chair and looked at her computer which silently reminded her that she had work to finish for her teaching job at a local university. It was hard to focus on writing when her thoughts keep going to the past in rhythm with the light walker's footsteps.

She clicked her fingers on the desk as she realised that, although he must still have been little more than a middle-aged man when she first saw him all those years ago, even then he'd seemed old. He must have been in his 70s by now, and while time had curved his spine, his walking pace was steady, even buoyant, like he was stepping on cushions of air instead of the hard road.

The old man seemed isolated on his walks, as if wearing blinkers inside an invisible bubble. Even if he'd once laughed and played as a child or ever felt carefree, there was no sign of it now. Years ago, Rebecca had tried to talk to him to say hello and introduce herself, feeling awkward about her height. His head only came up to her shoulders and he cringed away like a frightened cat, so she kept her distance after that.

Still, she felt linked to him. There was something oddly reassuring about his daily walks, something stable, locked in a routine and predictable, like the smell of coffee. He was as familiar as the silver-eyed crows, the thrushes chattering in the jacaranda trees and the fountain dancing inside OXI roundabout. Part of her looked out for him and felt relieved when he glided silently past her window day after day, his eyes on the hypnotic movement of the road passing underneath his feet.

Rebecca caught her distracted hazel eyes reflected in the computer screen and snapped back to attention. She needed to finish her latest research paper on parapsychology. It wouldn't write itself, and she hadn't yet packed for her trip to Greece. But her writing felt sluggish, and she wasn't happy with the few pages she'd produced. She crumpled them up and despaired of ever reaching the deadline.

Deciding to take a break, Rebecca drove to a bar near the US embassy where she knew some regulars, either from studying together or from working with them as colleagues. At the bar, she also kept up socially with her media contacts, who often featured her on their shows or in articles as a consultant psychologist.

The *Safe Haven* had been in the same location for decades. Two brothers had just taken it over and Rebecca was curious about the new owners, who'd kept the name unchanged. The bar's name was a nod to Cyprus' famous status as a haven for international spies and secret agencies, and was located near the massive, reinforced buildings housing the US and Russian embassies in Nicosia. The embassies faced each other from opposite sides of the road, their neighbourly proximity seeming to contradict the rivalry between the world powers, at least on the surface.

Ever since the end of the Cold War, there'd been an unspoken but closely observed agreement between the countries which had a presence in Cyprus: the island was neutral territory, and spies were off-limits, untouchable, invisible and anonymous. It was the worst-kept secret that when a wanted spy reached Cyprus, it seemed the local authorities would take a hands-off approach and turn a blind eye until the spy could reach a hideout.

On her way into the bar, Rebecca looked at the wall dedicated to the craft of spying. A photograph caught her eye, and she stopped in front of a suspected spy the authorities had recently arrested in Larnaca. Christopher Metsos, if indeed that was his name, was the most famous international spy case linked to the island and the American authorities suspected he was a deep undercover Russian agent. The Cypriot police had arrested him at Larnaca Airport after he was caught trying to enter the country with a stolen Canadian passport. Metsos paid his bail immediately, and the judge ordered him to show up daily at a police station instead of keeping him behind bars.

Was he a Russian spymaster? Rebecca ran her hand over her cropped blond hair and looked closely at the FBI photograph on the spy wall of fame. He didn't look like the risk-taking type and seemed ordinary with his Ray-Ban sunglasses, plain white V-neck sports shirt and well-kept grey moustache. The sole feature that stood out in his general aura of anonymity were expressionless blue eyes staring calmly back at the camera lens. Perhaps that was what had made him a good spook, at least before his photograph was plastered across the world press.

The mystery remained unsolved as far as Rebecca knew because he had never actually appeared at the police station. Instead, he had vanished with a sense of quiet efficiency and planning about his disappearance. He might have walked across the porous Green Line separating the north and south, or assumed a new identity and stayed in the country under everyone's noses. It was anyone's guess how many more covert operatives had escaped their hunters by taking refuge on the island.

The cool air inside the *Safe Haven* was a welcome relief from the heat and Rebecca inhaled the smell of spicy new wood shavings with quiet pleasure. The bar's wooden floor was walnut brown, and there were rows of clean glasses in shining stacks behind the bartender. Rebecca scanned the room but couldn't see anyone she knew, so she settled her light frame into a comfortable bar stool and ordered a glass of white wine.

"Are you from around here? You came to our opening a few days ago, but we didn't have time to talk," the barman said. He placed her drink on a coaster and his eyes wrinkled with a quick smile.

"Yes, I live 10 minutes away in the old city. My name is Rebecca Vassiliou."

"Nice to meet you, Rebecca, I'm Nick Solomou."

The tall bartender reached out a well-manicured hand to shake hers. As a psychologist, she noticed details about people. He'd chosen his pale-yellow linen shirt carefully, knowing it would flatter his brown eyes and compliment his tanned skin. Sculpted, wiry muscles on his arms, shoulders, and chest revealed his physical fitness, and she could only imagine how many hours he spent training to be in such peak shape. The bartender had a habit of running his hand across his chest muscles, enjoying the comforting sensation of linen sliding against the contours.

Rebecca didn't get a sense that he was interested in her or in any other woman in the bar except as a customer, so maybe he was gay. The bartender gave her a probing look before another smile spread across his face, camouflaging his sharp underlying curiosity. Rebecca caught the change in expression and her interest in him quickened.

"I just bought this place with my brother," Nick said.

"Yes, I heard. I'm glad you didn't change the name."

104

Nick flicked his hand. "Everyone already knows the name. It'd be foolish to change it."

Rebecca spilt wine on her skirt and flapped at the liquid with her hand. "That's cold."

Nick leaned over the bar to look at her skirt and gave her some soda water to wipe away the wine. "Don't worry, it won't stain. I like your clothes. Where do you buy them? I might know who designed your skirt."

He was keeping the conversation light-hearted, but she had a feeling there was more to him than met the eye, and played along with the small talk. "Thanks. You've got a good eye for style. Who do you think designed it?"

"It looks like an STS. Did Stelios design it?"

"Yes, you're right. It's from his new collection. I like to buy from artisan designers."

Nick gave her an appreciative look. "I bought my shirt from his boutique. I know Stelios. We dated years ago."

"How long were you together?" Rebecca said.

"Not long. Neither of us was looking for something serious."

"That's a shame. He's a good guy. Have you thought of looking him up again?"

Nick stretched. "No, that's all in the past. We're just friends now. Besides, I'm already taken and I'm happy with my partner. We've been together for about three years." His smile lit up the room. "We're talking about getting married now that the laws have relaxed towards same-sex unions."

Rebecca smiled back. "That's nice to hear. I'm still waiting for the right partner. Not that I mind being single. I've got plenty to do with my teaching job," she said.

Nick's expression was teasing. "A pretty woman like you, single? We'll have to find the right guy for you. Have you met my brother, Anastasios?"

"Not yet, but I'll look forward to it if he's as good looking as his brother," Rebecca teased him back.

Nick offered a mock bow at the return compliment and busied himself with bar chores, moving smoothly through the motions of stacking slices of lemon and lime. Suddenly, he put a martini shaker down on the bar as a thought struck him, and sent Rebecca another searching look which she met with a challenging one of her own.

"Rebecca, you said you live near the OXI roundabout, right? Have you ever seen an old man walking around the neighbourhood?"

Rebecca sipped her drink and raised her eyebrows at the random turn of conversation. Only a few hours ago, she had been watching the old man walk right past her window. Her favourite psychologist, Carl Jung, would have said the meeting with Nick was synchronicity in action. "I saw him earlier today, a thin man, right? It's odd you should ask me that. Do you know him?" she said.

Nick held her gaze. "Yes. His name is Alexandros Kyprianides. We just call him Alex. He's a distant relative." The barman broke eye contact. "Something terrible happened to him when he was a boy," he said.

Now that the conversation had turned serious, it confirmed her impression that there was more to Nick than light-hearted bar chat. "I'm sorry to hear that. It would explain why he never talks to anyone," Rebecca said. "I thought it was a psychological condition. What traumatized him?"

Nick stroked a finger on his forehead and pursed his mouth in thought. "It's a strange story. It goes back a long time to the 1940s when Alex was born," he said. "Everyone in the family knew he was a genius. But he didn't fit in, he made people uncomfortable."

Rebecca leaned forward on the bar. "Please tell me more, Nick. It's interesting."

He picked up the martini shaker and idled it back and forth in his hand. The ice clinked and rattled. "I can tell you what I know about Alex's teenage years. His parents were simple people," he said. "Both were uneducated. As far as I know, neither of them had ever left Nicosia and stayed in one place for their whole lives."

"What kind of genius was he?" Rebecca said.

"He was brilliant at maths. When Alex showed early signs of being so smart, they sent him away to study what he loved the most." Nick glanced sidelong at her. "It's not because they were bad people. They just had a problem communicating with him. They did the best they could," he said.

Rebecca's eyes were sympathetic. "I'm not surprised. It's a strain on the family. Child prodigies often need all their parents' attention and resources," she said.

Nick's shoulders relaxed and he grew more animated. "From the family stories, Alex was a burden on his parents," he said. "By the time he was 15, he preferred to spend most of his time at his tutor's house, just up the road from his parent's place in old Nicosia. I think his name was Georgiades."

Rebecca raised her eyebrows. "Did his parents tell him he was a prodigy and understand how unique their son was?"

Nick shrugged. "I doubt it. They were different times. There was trouble between the husband and wife and they fought constantly over money. Alex's abilities confused them," he said. "Back then, they stigmatized people who were different. It didn't help that Alex had problems communicating."

Rebecca's curiosity rose even further. "What do you remember about his abilities?" she said.

Nick tapped the shaker on the bar. "I wouldn't understand about maths," he said. "But my parents told me lots of stories about Alex's childhood. I remember a few about his education. There was a story about the first time Alex met his English benefactor, Sir James Merin."

Rebecca cocked her head. "An English patrician took an interest in your relative? That seems hard to believe. What connected them? I'd love to hear the story if you have the time."

Nick leaned forward on the bar and refilled her glass. "Why not? It's a quiet night. Let me see what I can remember. Alex's story goes back a long time."

The ambient noise in the bar faded into the distance as Nick told Alex's story. Every word he said took Rebecca back to another time and place, and she'd stayed until the early morning hours to hear the whole story. It was strange knowing the old man's real name after decades of calling him light walker.

The next day, Rebecca nearly missed her flight to Athens after she'd only had three hours of sleep. At the hotel, her tiredness and nerves about flying got her down for a moment. Ever since her parents had died in a plane accident, she'd had a phobia and for a moment at the hotel, the fatigue and heat got her down, but a quick shower soon revived her and she got dressed in a light blue linen suit and open-toed sandals for the class she'd be teaching later that day.

On the taxi ride to the university, the sight of the elegant columns around the Parthenon put her into a reflective state of mind. The constant honking of car horns amid the swerving traffic faded out as Rebecca mulled her upcoming lecture on the power of the mind. She had read and re-read Carl Jung's books a hundred times. The famous psychologist believed that fantasies are powerful because the mind can manifest them into present reality through synchronicity. Rebecca felt there was something magical about the ability to imagine something and then make it come alive and tangible in reality.

The conversation about Alex fascinated her, and snippets of Nick's story kept running through her memory, trying to make connections. How was it that a mathematics prodigy of such great talent that the British government wanted to employ him ended up as an isolated pensioner whose only activity was walking around the neighbourhood? What did it mean that she'd run into his distant relative in such a random setting as a bar? Rebecca didn't know why the old man fascinated her, but some instinct was urging her to find out more and she set her jaw as she resolved to go back to Nick's bar when she got home. She had more questions about his story because it sounded like a good study for her conference paper. The light walker's mystical tale was a long shot, but she needed a direction for the paper.

After her students had trickled in, Rebecca stood on the stage of the university's sound-proofed lecture hall and looked at the small group sitting on blue chairs fixed in rows. "How many of you believe in parapsychology?" she said.

Three or four students put their hands up and the rest of them looked away or chuckled. A few of them curled their lips or shook their heads. Rebecca pointed to one student who had put up her hand. "Go ahead and tell us your name and story. Why do you believe in parapsychology?" she said.

The student was tall and built like an athlete. She was around 24 years old and wore blue jeans, sandals, and a black t-shirt. She'd perched designer sunglasses on her straight, natural honey-brown hair. "My name is Polytimi. My grandmother says she can read coffee grounds and tell the future. All of our family members go to her for advice," she said.

Rebecca gave her an encouraging look. "How accurate are her readings?" she said.

The student hesitated and fidgeted with her hair while looking at the others, afraid they'd judge her or think she was crazy.

"It's okay, go ahead, we're just talking here. I know it's an unusual topic," Rebecca said.

"Everything she says comes true. My yiayia predicted my mother's pregnancies," Polytimi said. "She helped my uncle beat cancer by warning him to go to the doctor, and she can see things happening in other countries, places she's never visited in her life, just by touching something that belongs to a stranger. She has visions."

Several of the other students gasped and shuffled their feet. Rebecca snapped her fingers. "What you've described is an outstanding example of precognition and clairvoyance," she said. "How many of you know of someone who reads coffee grounds and uses their readings to predict events?"

This time, most of the students raised their hands. Rebecca switched on a projector. "Physical phenomena can explain authentic clairvoyance if you think widely enough."

"What do you mean?" Polytimi said.

"Quantum physics is the study of subatomic particles and waves. I think of it as an invisible ocean of mysterious particles which connects everything and everyone far beyond what we can imagine," Rebecca said. She clicked the remote control, switching to an image of the Pacific Ocean.

"It's impossible to know how many subatomic particles there are all around us," she said. "We can think of it as an invisible ocean connecting everything. What if some people are more sensitive to this ocean of particles than others?"

The next slide showed a man deep in meditation. "Perhaps their brains have adapted in ways that allow them to connect to information that other people can't perceive," Rebecca said. "Maybe it's easier for them to access the collective consciousness at different points in time and understand reality in a new way. Exploring this idea is part of parapsychology."

Rebecca gave Polytimi a penetrating look. "That could explain why your grandmother knows everything about her family's present, past, and future," she said. "Scientists have already proven there is quantum activity in our brains. That means that we're all connected to the ocean of particles I described before but the fact is, no one has concrete proof of the connection between the quantum field and parapsychology."

The students were all ears for the rest of the lecture. Although the academic world didn't consider parapsychology to be a hard science, the topic captivated Rebecca's students because most people have come across inexplicable phenomena in their lives.

After the lecture, it was time for Rebecca's favourite exercise. "We're going to split up into two groups: the believers and the sceptics," she said.

The students shuffled over into two separate groups and Rebecca walked down the steps and stood between them. "The believers will take the side of Carl Jung and William James, who wrote about different realities and synchronicities," she said. "The sceptics will argue against the believers. The team that wins the debate will make the most valid and relevant points. Assign a speaker. You have one minute each, and there are two rounds."

Polytimi ended up in the believer group and spoke first, gripping the back of a chair. "The psychologist William James wrote that our brains could detect the existence of things beyond obvious limits, things like different realities," she said. "Carl Jung noticed mysterious synchronicities that rule our lives and destinies. They understood that our reality is a malleable, ever-changing fluctuation of events and coincidences. Parapsychology is real, we just haven't proved it yet."

She sat down, clasping her shaking hands together and a short lad called Andreas stood to attention. "Dr Joseph Banks Rhine and Uri Geller had plenty of chances to prove that telekinesis and clairvoyance exist," he said. "They've never proved it. So far, their theories are nothing more than dust in the wind."

Polytimi renewed her grip on the chair in front of her as she stood up again. "We don't invest enough money in studying quantum consciousness," she said. "The scientific world spent billions on the Large Hadron Collider to discover the Higgs Boson particle. Why not put more money into studying quantum activity and how it powers our consciousness? Until we take parapsychology seriously, we can't know for sure that it doesn't exist."

Andreas leapt to his feet. "That would be wasted money. Consciousness is not a thing to rely on for science," he said.

"Scientific inquiry discovers new things by following laboratory protocols and proof. Discoveries don't just float around in the quantum field like butterflies."

Andreas puffed his chest out even further. "Until there's hard evidence, the scientific world can't take parapsychology seriously," he said, sitting back down.

Polytimi hesitated, rubbing the back of her neck. "When my mother was pregnant with me, my yiayia told my parents not to take Flight 715 to Cyprus," she said. "Thank God they listened to her. The flight crashed into the sea with no survivors. If it weren't for her prediction, I wouldn't be here today to debate whether our minds have extraordinary abilities or not."

A hush fell over the room. Rebecca felt frozen for a moment, then covered her throat with her palm. "My parents died on that flight. This is more than coincidence," she said.

Andreas' chest deflated, and he muttered under his breath. Rebecca rolled her shoulders to shake off the sudden excitement of synchronicity. "Well done, class, win or lose, the debate was excellent. You'll receive extra credits for participating," she said, moving back to the lecturer's stage.

"As the debate has shown us, we can't directly see the proof of clairvoyance and similar phenomena," Rebecca said. "We don't have the technology to prove them in a laboratory setting. We can only perceive them indirectly in real-life stories. Any questions?"

After the lecture, Polytimi invited Rebecca to meet her clairvoyant grandmother and she accepted, excited at the chance to learn more about her psychic abilities. Their village was a stone's throw away from Athens in the beautiful, peaceful countryside. The view was ethereal; rounded foothills and the pale cerulean sky resounded with an ancient power. Lulled by the rocking of the car, Rebecca imagined mythological Greek gods and ancient philosophers walking across the hills, like the massive rays of light and shadows chasing each other along the surfaces of the slopes.

When they reached the village house, they stooped down so that Maro Theanides could greet them with a kiss on each cheek. She was a short woman but seemed taller because of her erect posture and direct, calm gaze. As Polytimi introduced them, Rebecca had the impression that if the Parthenon statues were to come to life, this was how they'd look at her, with a suggestion of infinity in their eyes.

Maro smiled at Rebecca. "Sit, sit," she said in Greek, waving her towards the kitchen table. She wore her hair up in a bun and wore a buttoned-up black dress with a collar. The dress reached her ankles, which were encased in sturdy black shoes. A slim watch nestled in a soft fold of fat on her forearm and a gold wedding band glowed on her ring finger.

"Thank you." Rebecca said as she sat at the wooden table on a traditional woven chair.

More rapid-fire Greek followed, and Polytimi translated because the village slang was difficult to understand. Rebecca's mixed parentage meant that her spoken Greek was good enough, but the ancient language was rich with dialects it took a lifetime to learn.

"My grandmother says she'll read your coffee grounds," Polytimi said.

"Can she explain how her readings work?"

"Yiayia says it's as natural as breathing. When she reads them, powerful images come to her mind. She even hears voices."

"And does she hear the same voices after the reading is over?"

"No, they're different each time," Polytimi said.

"When did she first find out about her abilities?"

"It started when she was about 12 years old. It was difficult at first, but now everyone believes her because the visions always come true."

The shadows in the kitchen grew longer as the sun headed towards the horizon. Rebecca's coffee arrived, and as she drank it, she smelled spices and earth in the silty, hot liquid. Maro tipped Rebecca's small white cup onto its saucer. Ten minutes passed as they chatted in the cosy kitchen with savoury smells wafting from three saucepans bubbling away on the stovetop.

Maro carefully turned the cup the right way up and studied the shapes formed by the finely-ground coffee. The coffee shapes looked like brown cobwebs and Rebecca couldn't make heads or tails of them. Slowly, the coffee grounds rose out of the cup and floated in front of them in a lacy pattern. In the silence, Rebecca focused on the clairvoyant's uncanny orange-brown eyes, which were filled with the infinity she'd sensed earlier. She felt lost in those eyes, as if floating in space,

116

and her shoulders tensed as the coffee grounds circled over the table.

"Grandmother says you recently met a man who will become important to your work," Polytimi whispered. "A spirit voice told her that grave danger lies in old wounds. Beware of the evil one who plots against the land. Protect yourself and protect the light walker from harm."

The kitchen seemed to darken and Rebecca felt her heart beating faster as she drew a quick breath to calm down. "How could you possibly know about the light walker? I haven't told anyone about his nickname," she said.

"Yiayia said she has an image of him in her mind. He's an old man who walks past you every day."

Grandmother Maro waved her hand and a ghostly light walker floated through the air above the kitchen table. Rebecca saw Alex's figure suspended in mid-air with a blazing rainbow shape next to him, together with what appeared to be black space and stars around the bodies made of light. Her jaw dropped, but Maro and Polytimi didn't blink an eye.

"My God, her gift is amazing. What does she mean by the evil one?" Rebecca said, holding back excitement and a pang of fear.

Polytimi asked her grandmother in Greek. "My grandmother sees visions of a white-haired woman standing in a river of blood. She appears to her like a statue made of ice," she translated.

The sharp smell of coffee wafted towards Rebecca as the floating grounds from her cup collapsed onto the table in a cloud of fine dust.

"I don't understand," Rebecca said.

"That's all yiayia can tell you. She feels the woman in her vision is ominous and has bad energy, that she's a threat. Her visions don't come with explanations. She senses them more than anything else," Polytimi said.

Rebecca waited for more information from grandmother Maro, who simply brushed the coffee grounds off the table, picked up the cup and went back to cooking lunch, which turned out to be the creamy and satisfying dish, moussaka. They ate together at the kitchen table and washed their food down with a glass of Malagouzia, one of Rebecca's favourite local dry white wines. Maro and Polytimi gave her warm hugs when she left, and they promised to see her whenever she was in Athens.

After their goodbyes, Rebecca went back to Athens to catch her flight home. The short plane ride gave her a chance to make some notes about the fascinating visit with the clairvoyant. The questions buzzed and circled in her mind and reality suddenly seemed as disconnected as the dome of the sky and the tiny dots of the Greek islands far below the plane.

To overcome her flying phobia, Rebecca distracted herself by making rapid notes on her laptop. Some clairvoyants derived information from energetic vibrations, she remembered from her research. Somehow, their minds could reach beyond the limits of their brainwaves to ride other energies to faraway places.

118

How was the old lady able to communicate with a stranger's experiences through the coffee grounds? Did she sense an energetic echo from Rebecca's touch on the cup? Did the energy in Rebecca's mind create patterns in the coffee that meant something to her? How on earth did the apparition in the old lady's kitchen transform itself from floating coffee grounds, and what did the illusion of the light walker mean?

Rebecca's research had revealed some fascinating and unexpected things, but there was a big question mark around precognition. Maro had never met her before, so even if she were adept at reading characters, it wouldn't explain how she knew something so specific about her life in another country.

And as for the reference to a woman with evil intentions, Rebecca didn't know what it meant, but given the clairvoyant's insight into the light walker's presence in her life, she'd probably encounter her in the future and she felt a faint dread at the thought.

For the rest of the week, Rebecca buckled down to write her conference paper, following the instinct that kept pushing her to find out more about Alex's background. Since the clairvoyant had envisioned the light walker in her life, there was an obvious connection between him and parapsychology, so on Friday night, Rebecca went back to see Nick at the *Safe Haven* bar. He was at the door, pinning a photograph on the spy wall of fame. When she peered at the picture of a blond woman with icy blue eyes, Rebecca felt something walk over her grave and shuddered. "Who is that woman?" she said.

Nick's smile took on a bitter twist. "Meet Lady Regina Addington."

"Regina? The woman who tried to drown Alex when he was a boy?"

"The one and only. Doesn't she look like a witch?" Nick said.

Rebecca nodded. "She looks cold and frightening. I've seen similar expressions in people with no conscience," she said.

"Come in. I'd like you to meet someone," Nick said.

After serving her a glass of white wine, he introduced her to his attractive, green-eyed boyfriend, Costas and they sat together at Rebecca's table. Costas was dressed as stylishly as Nick and favoured a more bohemian style; the designer had embroidered his shirt with a blue and green pattern that suited his eyes.

"What kind of work do you do?" Costas asked as Nick served the drinks.

"I'm a psychologist," Rebecca said.

"That sounds interesting. Tell us more."

The bar was half full, and the warm sound of people socializing buzzed in the background. Rebecca raised her voice over the noise. "It's fascinating. My master's degree is in psychology and my doctorate is in parapsychology. I'm teaching now."

"And what does parapsychology mean?" Costas said.

"My research is on clairvoyance, telepathy, and precognition. When I was in Athens, a clairvoyant showed me a vision of Nick's relative, Alexandros," she said.

"OK, wow, that's a lot. So spooky," Costas said with a nervous laugh.

"I could tell you some stories, I've come across a lot of spooky things" Rebecca said. She looked at Nick. "Speaking of stories, would you tell me more about Regina?"

"She married a wealthy lord and had a daughter called Charlotte," Nick said. "She comes and goes from north Nicosia, from what I've heard. If she were caught on our side, she'd be arrested."

"What do you know about her daughter?" Rebecca said.

"Rumour has it that she's unhinged, like her mother," Nick said. "Remember Stelios, the designer? She's his client and treats him like absolute dirt, takes forever to pay him. It's not like she's short of money."

"Perhaps her mother's twisted her. We know she's capable of it after what she did to Alex," Rebecca said.

"Do you know why Alex is still so withdrawn? It happened when he was a boy, he's an old man now," Costas said.

"It's possible he has an underlying condition. Asperger's Syndrome might explain Alex's behaviour," Rebecca said, sipping her wine. "Sometimes, their hearing is also sensitive to the point that even soft noises can disturb them."

"You could be right, you're the expert. But as far as I know, there's no official diagnosis," Nick said.

"Can you tell me more about Alex's background. I understand the big picture, but I'd love to hear more. I'm thinking of researching his life. Perhaps there's a parapsychological angle, not a pathological one," Rebecca said.

Nick's hand clenched. "All I know is that Regina destroyed his life," he said.

"Are you okay? You seem upset," Rebecca said.

"I hate that woman," Nick blurted out.

Costas covered Nick's fist with his hand. "I understand that, but it happened a long time ago. Regina must be an old woman now," he said.

"It doesn't make her any less dangerous. She has her daughter and her husband's money to help her," Nick said.

"She seems to have it in for Cyprus," Costas said.

Rebecca leaned forward and met Nick's eyes. "You understand that's what she wants, right?" she said.

Nick frowned. "What do you mean?"

"She wants people to be confused and angry. If you're hurt and weak, that's how she gets what she needs," Rebecca said.

Nick glared at her. "My family has a reward for her arrest or any information about her. She won't get what she wants," he said.

Rebecca held his gaze calmly and Nick put his hand to his mouth. "Oh my God, I'm so sorry," he said. "It's not your fault or even your problem. It's just that you look..."

"English?" she said.

Nick dropped his gaze. "I'm sorry."

Rebecca smiled and sipped her wine. "Don't worry about it. I know it's not personal. If I hear anything about Regina, I'll be sure to let you know," she said.

The next day, Rebecca had coffee on Ledra Street with her friend and fellow psychologist, Marina Avramidou. The central shopping street was in a pedestrian zone with faded red, yellow and orange sunshades blocking the sun's rays. Marina wore white shorts and an orange t-shirt with a belt around her curvy waist and the bangles on her arm jingled and clinked together with each movement.

In June, the island filled with two million tourists, more than double the number of residents. They watched tour groups with rucksacks, water bottles and ice-creams flock to the infamous Green Line that divided Nicosia between the Greek-Cypriot and Turkish-Cypriot communities. The Green Line was the military symbol of division, but the tourists were blissfully unaware of the many more unseen rifts and splits that ran like an undercurrent through the city.

The friends sipped fragrant coffees, reminding Rebecca of the clairvoyant in Greece. "Do you know anyone who reads coffee cups?" she said as they watched the tourists walking up Ledra Street.

Marina flicked her hand and her bracelets jangled. "A few, but they're all liars. I don't believe a word of what they say. They always tell me I'll have money soon, but so far, no luck," she said with a laugh.

Rebecca nodded. "Most of them are liars and fraudsters, I agree. I met an exception to the rule the other day. I think I found an authentic clairvoyant in a village just outside Athens."

"Really? Who is she?"

"Her name is Maro, and she read my coffee grounds. She seems to be a clairvoyant, based on what she told me about my life. She saw things she couldn't possibly have known about me. It was uncanny and I might use the experience for my paper."

Marina's eyes lit up. "Finally! I'm glad you found inspiration. How's your writing going?"

Rebecca shrugged. "It's not going at all. I keep discarding ideas, but I hope this one will develop into something worth writing about."

"I'm sure you'll find the right way to prove that parapsychology exists. What direction are you taking?" Marina said.

"I'm researching an old man with strange connections to parapsychology," Rebecca said. "I call him light walker. From the stories I've heard, he's either a powerful mystic or completely deluded, I'm not sure which."

"Has he seen a psychiatrist?" Marina said.

Rebecca nearly knocked over her coffee in excitement. "You're a genius! Yes, Nick told me that he saw a Dr Simons in Oxford. I could look him up," she said. They smiled at each other. "The coffee's on me," Rebecca said as she called the waiter over to pay.

It only took Stella a few hours to learn that Dr. Simons, had died in 1972 but she was relieved to find out that his son Philip, who was also a psychologist, was alive. It was a chance to go deeper into Alex's past and she called his number. "Doctor, hello, my name is Rebecca. I'm interested in a patient your father saw in 1955, a young boy called Alexandros Kyprianides."

"Hello, Rebecca. That was a long time ago. Why do you want to know?" Philip said.

"It's research for a psychology conference at my university."

"Alexandros was an interesting case. My father couldn't diagnose what was disturbing the boy, but he often talked about it. They only sat together for a short time, and Alexandros refused to speak," Philip said.

"Is there anything you remember, something that stands out? No matter how far-fetched, it'd help my research."

"There was one strange thing. My father only told me about the incident because he didn't want people to think he was imagining things."

Rebecca's head snapped up in anticipation. People who encounter parapsychological activity often hide their experiences out of embarrassment or fear that others will think they're crazy. "What was out of the ordinary?" she said.

"My father said that Alexandros didn't speak verbally. He spoke with his mind. You might say he used telepathy to send mind pictures into the air, like mirages," Philip said.

"Yes, I've heard about this power. What were the pictures about?" Rebecca said.

"Some of them were about events that hadn't yet happened. My father recognised the images when they were broadcast during the 1955 war. There were others from the 1960s and 70s," Philip said. "The image my father never forgot was a vicious attempt to drown the boy in a pond. He had nightmares about it for years after he met Alexandros."

"Did you know that the attempted drowning happened in reality, and Alexandros nearly died after the attack?" Rebecca said.

"Well, no, he didn't know that it actually took place. There was no way my father could have known about it outside of the visions."

Something in his voice caught Rebecca's attention, it seemed he was avoiding a straight answer. "Did your father know Sir James Merin?" she said.

"No, they didn't know each other, but he knew of the family through Dr Carter. Leo and my father were close friends."

After that, Philip refused to be drawn any further and they said their goodbyes. The puzzle expanded in Rebecca's mind as she concentrated on writing a new outline for her paper. A few hours later, her cell phone rang.

"I'm looking for Rebecca Vassiliou," a crisp, English voice said.

"Rebecca speaking, who is this?"

"My name is Sam Carter."

"Sam Carter... Are you related to Leo Carter, a mathematics professor I heard about recently?" Rebecca said.

"Yes, I'm his son. Dr Simons just called me and told me about your conversation. I must warn you to stop asking questions. It's not safe," Sam said.

Rebecca's hand tightened on the phone. "What do you mean?" she said.

"Trust me. It could be dangerous."

"I don't even know you. What's this all about? Are you threatening me?" But the line had gone silent, he'd already disconnected the call.

Rebecca ignored the mysterious warning and worked on her research. Her drive to find proof of parapsychology grew stronger as she wrote her notes because Alex's story promised parapsychological facts about telepathy, clairvoyance, and the power of a spiritual protector.

As she wrote, she remembered that during the reading of her coffee grounds, Maro had said it was important to help the light walker as much as she could. Alex believed he had met an entity made of light that protected him. The question was, what effect- if any - did the light walker's mental energy have on the natural world around him?

The proof was tantalizingly out of reach, and it all depended on Alex's mental state. She had to work out several complex questions. Were his parapsychological experiences real, and did he meet a light being? Or was his behaviour caused by a psychological condition like Asperger's Syndrome or schizophrenia? Could quantum activity explain Alex's telepathy? Were there beings of conscious light who balance the multi-verse and communicate in ways she couldn't yet understand? And if they existed, how would they connect with the quantum field?

Frustrated, Rebecca pushed her chair away from her desk as she felt the pressure of these massive questions getting to her. She took a few deep breaths to calm down and drove to the *Safe Haven*, hoping that Nick was in a good mood so she could ask more questions. But he wasn't there and instead, a different bartender caught her eye with a wink and walked over to her holding a menu. Rebecca breathed in the bar's familiar spicy smell of fresh wood shavings and another scent, a combination of violet and sandalwood, that she realised belonged to the barman.

"Would you like a drink? A glass of wine, perhaps?" he said.

"Yes, a glass of Malagouzia would be great, thanks. Is Nick working tonight?" Rebecca said.

"He might come in later. I'm his brother, Anastasios. We bought this place together. Did you know that I'm 35 years old today? Let me buy you the first one."

"Happy birthday!" Rebecca smiled at him, and he winked at her again with a cheeky grin. She gave him a cool look, and he toned down his flirtatious behaviour. "Sorry about winking at you. Don't take it wrong. It's just my way of being friendly," he said.

She looked up at him from underneath her eyelashes. "That's okay, at least you thought you were charming," she said.

Anastasios smiled at the banter, and she thought to herself that his interest in her could prove to be a massive help if he knew as much about Alex as his brother did. It didn't hurt that he was easy on the eyes, tall with broad, solid shoulders and an athlete's narrow hips. The women must throw themselves at him.

"My name's Rebecca. Maybe he told you about sharing the story of your relative, Alexandros, with me. I've been following up with Nick for my research."

"Yes, you're the psychologist who's writing a paper, Nick told me you'd been talking," Anastasios said, hooking his thumbs into the waist of his black jeans in a classic male mating posture. As a psychologist, she knew his body language was flirtatious, but she couldn't help blushing and touching her neck in an automatic response.

I like him, but I don't have the time to flirt.

Rebecca finished her drink and set off home. As she walked towards her car, she felt the evening air drift by softly, cooling her skin. She strolled along the dark road, stepping in pools of orange light from the streetlamps. A shadow on the side of the road caught her peripheral vision but vanished too quickly for her to see what it was, and she shook her head, dismissing a sudden surge of fear.

Rebecca parked near her house and walked along the shadowy Xanthis Xenierou Street towards her front door, thinking about Sam Carter's phone call. She wondered what he meant by his warning and her muscles tensed up as she thought about everything she'd learned about the light walker. It was another coincidence that, as a child, she'd nicknamed Alex with the same name as his spirit consciousness - Phos, the Light Walker. Both roads led to the same place – an enigma.

Just as she slipped the key into her front door, she heard a sound behind her and whirled around. A heavy body crushed her against the door. She smelled acrid sweat as her attacker stifled her. Rebecca tried to glimpse his face. The man was featureless until she realised he was wearing a mask. He gripped her throat, cutting off her air. Rebecca choked on her scream. She struggled to break free. Her survival instinct took over, and she used her height to fight back. She clutched at his balaclava over her shoulder. Her thumb dug into his eye, making him shout in pain. The balaclava fell off his face and neck, and she spotted a black tattoo in the shape of a claw holding a globe. The tattoo whipped out of view when he forced her to the ground on her stomach.

The man gave a visceral grunt, his knee in the small of her back. "If you see me again, it'll be the last thing you ever see. Don't make me come back. Stop asking questions about the Merin family."

Chapter 9

The sharp pain in her back made Rebecca's voice suddenly come back and she screamed as loudly as she could. She heard footsteps pounding on the pavement and another man shouted from a few meters away. "Get away from her!"

The thug turned his head, giving Rebecca the chance to slither out of his grasp before letting out another scream and collapsing on the road. After one last black look, her attacker ran away, disappearing into the night as Rebecca's tears blurred his hulking back.

"Can you stand, are you alright?" Rebecca's rescuer said.

She couldn't stand and her legs shook too much when she tried, so he sat down next to her on the pavement. The man was tall and blond, in his late twenties. Fair eyebrows knitted over his blue eyes as he peered into hers. "We talked earlier on the phone. I'm Sam Carter, Leo Carter's son. I tried to warn you about the dangers you face," he said.

She blinked at him as the memory of their phone call trickled back into her stunned brain. "Leo Carter... yes, Alex's maths professor from Oxford?"

"That's right, how did you know?"

Rebecca held her bruised neck. "I've been researching him. What are you doing here, aren't you from England?" she said.

Sam looked at her in concern. "Yes, but I live here. Do you need a doctor?" he said.

Rebecca broke down, clutching her stomach as she cried. Sam moved closer to her and placed a warm hand on her shoulder, reminding her of her mother's caring hand when she'd soothed her as a child. Once, she had come running home from school in a fright after some bigger boys had bullied her in the playground. She'd slipped and fallen on the gravel while she was running away, and her knee was bleeding from a deep gash. Her mother's hug and gentle touch calmed her as she cleaned the gash and put a plaster on it. No matter what childhood scrapes she got into, her mother could always kiss it better, the familiar smell of cigarettes and musky perfume soothing her.

Rebecca cried harder at the thought of missing her mother's presence in her life and Sam quickly removed his hand from her shoulder. "Sorry, did I hurt you?" he said.

"It's not you."

"Rebecca, I live close by in the old city. Would you like to come home with me for a cup of tea? My mother's there and she can take care of you. It's not safe for you to be alone, and I need to tell you why you were attacked."

"Do you know who it was?" she said in a wavering voice.

"I don't know his identity, but I know he assaulted you to intimidate you and stop you asking so many questions."

132

"I need something from my flat, give me a minute," she said. Once inside, Rebecca trembled her way through a glass of wine while Sam waited outside. She noticed a printout of her research notes on the desk and wondered whether it was worth going ahead with the paper. She couldn't understand why a harmless, introverted old man stirred up so much aggression. Was it worth pursuing the truth about Alex Kyprianides?

Rebecca decided to trust Sam and walked with him through the warren of ancient city streets towards the Archbishop's Palace in the heart of the old city. The streets were so narrow they barely fitted one car and the houses loomed over them as they walked side by side. When they reached his house, a tall, elderly woman opened the door. She had a gentle smile and wore a pearl necklace.

"Rebecca, this is my mother, Willow," Sam said.

"Willow? The name sounds familiar," Rebecca said.

"Why? Have we met?" Willow said.

"The name came up in some research I'm doing. She was the wife of an ex-governor of Cyprus, Sir James Merin," Rebecca said.

"Ex-wife. Before she divorced him, my mother was married to James. She later married my father, Leo," Sam said.

"I see, so you're the same woman I heard about in Alex's story. Pleased to meet you."

Willow patted Rebecca's shoulder. "Come in, Rebecca. I understand you've had a frightening experience. We have some difficult things to talk about," she said.

They sat in the kitchen at an inviting oak table in one of Nicosia's beautiful old homes. Fans set high in the ceiling gently moved the humid air and Rebecca was attracted by the atmosphere in the room. The Carters had made elegant arrangements of antique furniture and ornaments around their home. Fine art adorned the walls and soft lighting brought out the reds, greens, and blues of the sculptures and ceramics on the tables scattered around the room.

Willow's hands trembled as she set down a cup of tea on the table in front of Rebecca, who wasn't sure if it was age or fear causing her hands to shake. There was a faint scent of rose perfume in the air.

"Philip told us you're writing a paper about Alexandros Kyprianides. I must ask you to stop," Willow said.

Rebecca looked at her under lowered eyebrows. "Why should I?"

"There are things you don't understand about the situation that involve my daughter, Regina," Willow said.

Rebecca couldn't help the note of bitterness in her voice. "That's not good enough, Willow. I've been through a lot to find out more about Alex, and I've got the bruises to prove it. I already know Regina tried to drown Alex when he was a boy," she said.

Willow and Sam exchanged looks. "After Oliver's suicide, Regina became more vindictive," Willow said. "She sued James for her trust fund even though she would have received it anyway. On top of that, her husband owns half of

England and mining rights in the ex-colonies, so it wasn't about the money."

"Her behaviour fits the profile of the dark triad in psychology. Even as a young woman she was abusive verbally and physically from what I understand. If that's the case, she lacks empathy and is determined to win at all costs," Rebecca said.

"I don't know what you psychologists would call it, but things are much worse than you think," Willow said.

Sam jumped in to say: "Regina and her husband run an extremist group of provocateurs called Reclamation. It's an underground organisation supported by people with a lot of money. Using violence is their first resort and they're determined to exploit everyone around them."

"Reclamation is fanatical about taking over resources that belong to ex-colonies," Willow said. "They want the mining rights to Cyprus's natural resources, and they don't care what they have to do to get them."

Rebecca looked from mother to son. "Again, this sounds like anti-social behaviour, in my opinion. The disregard for the rights of others is a red flag. Are you in contact with Regina?"

Willow fidgeted with her necklace. "No, we haven't spoken for years. I don't even know where she is. She hates me for marrying another man and having his child."

Rebecca touched the angry bruises on her neck again and her mouth went dry. "I still don't understand why that thug attacked me tonight," she said.

Sam grimaced. "Nasty business. Did you notice any marks on the man who attacked you?"

"Yes, on his neck there was a tattoo."

Sam handed Rebecca a drawing of a tattoo. "Did it look like this?"

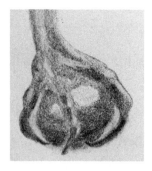

"Yes, that's it. What does it mean?"

"That's Reclamation's symbol. Its members all have the same tattoo. They want to claw back oil and gold worth billions of pounds from former colonies, starting with Cyprus," Sam said.

Willow drew a shaky breath. "The only thing Regina fears is exposure. My daughter has done some terrible things. Trying to drown Alex all those years ago was just the beginning. You can't imagine what I've been through."

Rebecca's eyes welled up. "Since you know full well what's going on, why don't you go to the police? Some mercenary just tried to strangle me because of Regina's games," she said.

Willow blinked at the anger in Rebecca's voice and straightened her spine, taking a deep breath as her strength came back. "There's already an arrest warrant out for her," she said. "Not all my children are bad seeds, remember that Sam tried to warn you, Rebecca. My son has stood by his family, and he's tried to help you too."

Sam put his hand on his mother's shoulder. "Regina and her husband have enough money to enlist and control hundreds of cohorts. When the police arrest the man who attacked you, he won't know anything other than his orders," he said.

Willow nodded. "Regina's careful not to meet the rank-and-file."

"Why come after me?" Rebecca said.

"If you write about Alexandros, her story will come out, too. It would tip her over the last edge. God knows what she and her family would do next, we've seen what they're capable of," Willow said.

Rebecca breathed deeply to calm down. "I understand now that attacking me is a way to put pressure on you. I'm sorry, Willow. Where are you getting your information about Reclamation?"

Mother and son looked at each other again. "We have an inside source," Sam said.

Rebecca thought quickly through the possibilities. "Is it Philip Simons Jr?" She saw by their expressions that she was right, but they stayed silent and loyal to their friend.

"Does Regina know about Alex's mystical abilities? He believes a supernatural force protects him," Rebecca said.

Sam scoffed. "She wouldn't care. She's not the imaginative type, just the manipulative type. Regina tried to have me expelled by lying about me to the Dean when I was studying physics at Oxford. Luckily, he saw right through her."

Rebecca took another deep breath. "I'll have to think about the situation. It won't solve anything to back down now and my work's important to me," she said.

"Surely you can see it's dangerous to publish Alex's story," Willow said.

Rebecca's expression was rueful. "That may be so, but what about the cost to me and my work? Am I going to spend the future waiting for the next attack? I don't want to look over my shoulder for the rest of my life," she said.

Willow sighed. "Please think about it. I urge you to find another topic for your research, otherwise the rest of your life might be shorter than you think."

Rebecca slapped her hand on the table. "I don't accept threats!"

"My mother isn't threatening you; she's protecting you. She knows Regina only too well. She's ruthless," Sam said.

Rebecca crossed her arms and gritted her teeth, ignoring Sam's calming hand motions. She pushed her chair back and stood. "So you keep telling me, what am I supposed to do, go into hiding?"

"I know you're in shock, Rebecca, but this is not a theory. Please take it seriously. Regina's deadly and she's got a lot of power," Willow said. "I'm sorry you stumbled into a nest of vipers."

As Rebecca stood to leave, Sam handed over her jacket and she snatched it from his hands. "I need to talk to someone. I'll call you," she said, slamming the door on her way out.

A few hours later, she was still fuming and clicking her fingertips on the desk in her flat while forcing herself to make notes about the situation and plan her next move. Writing everything out helped calm her mind and she leaned back in her chair, wondering if Sir James was still in England and whether he could give her more information about Alex. She found the UK number for a James Merin in Oxford and as she picked up her phone to make the call, Rebecca crossed her fingers that it was the man she was looking for and that he was still alive.

"Merin speaking," a man said in a quavering voice.

Rebecca realised he must be well into his nineties by now. "Hello, Sir James. I'm a Doctor of Psychology in Cyprus doing research on Alexandros Kyprianides, do you remember him?"

Sir James sounded surprised. "Yes, I remember him, the Cypriot mathematics prodigy. He's the subject of your research? What do you want to know?" he said in a firmer tone.

"If my information is correct, back in the 1950s, he was about to be shot by a British soldier before you intervened," Rebecca said. "Alexandros believes that a mystical force worked through him to influence you to save his life so he could carry out a mission to protect Cyprus' independence."

"Poppycock," came the abrupt answer.

"Then why did you stop the soldier from murdering him? What were you doing that day?" Rebecca said.

"Patrol inspections. And my ex-wife Willow confessed to me about the vile thing my children did to him. After that, I felt it was my duty to protect Alexandros. I warned the patrols in old Nicosia to leave him be."

"Have you helped him or been in touch with him since the war with EOKA?" Rebecca said.

"No, I haven't been back to Cyprus since then. That's all in the past for me. Willow has lived there since our divorce, though. She probably knows more about Alexandros' life," Sir James said.

Halfway through her thanks, the line went dead as Sir James hung up abruptly without saying goodbye. Rebecca sighed. "Definitely a point for the sceptics," she muttered.

Her next call was to Willow Carter. "Willow, I've decided to go ahead with my research on Alex's powers. I won't let Regina's organisation intimidate me," she said.

There was a long pause. "You'd best come back over, Rebecca," Willow said.

At the Carter's kitchen table, Willow smoothed white strands of hair off her face with hands gnarled from arthritis. "So, you're still pursuing this dangerous course?" she said.

"Yes, I'm sorry if it disturbs you, but if I stop now, Regina will win the war of intimidation, and things will only get worse," Rebecca said.

Willow looked down at the table and shook her head as an elderly man walked into the kitchen. Heavy-lidded, mischievous brown eyes met Rebecca's and lit up with an impish smile.

"Rebecca, this is my husband, Leo Carter."

Leo shook her hand. "It's a pleasure to meet you. I've heard a lot about you, Rebecca."

Willow's face looked drawn. "I don't feel well. I'm going to lie down. Leo can tell you what you need to know," she said, standing up.

Leo's caring touch on her waist brought back a faint smile to her lips and she left the kitchen with a lighter step. While Rebecca sipped her tea, Leo joined her at the table with a glass of single malt. "You're a determined young lady. I admire your courage and hope you have the wisdom to be careful," he said.

Rebecca clenched her hand; she'd had enough of the warnings. "I appreciate your concern, Leo, but I can take care of myself. Please tell me what you know about Alex's delusions or mystical powers, whatever you call them."

Leo sipped the whiskey as he gathered his thoughts. The kitchen was so quiet that Rebecca heard his throat click as he swallowed his drink. "Alex used to conjure up the most astonishing illusions when he was my student. That's why I'm half-inclined to believe in my friend's quests and his claim of mystical powers," he said.

Rebecca sat back and crossed her arms. "I'm still in two minds about Alex's powers," she said. "I've spoken with James

Merin and he said it was nonsense that Alex had a spirit protector. He told me he tried to look after Alex because his twins had attempted to drown him."

Leo tutted and shook his head. "James's a practical man, not a man of imagination or one to wallow in sentiment. He buried his son's suicide as fast as he could because he couldn't bear the pain and had to draw a line under the past," he said.

"Yet you're a man of science, a mathematician."

"If there's one thing I've learned about mathematics, the more you know about numbers, the more mystical they become," Leo said with a laugh.

Rebecca's mobile phone rang, interrupting their conversation.

"I warned you to stay away," a harsh voice said when Rebecca picked up.

The hard tone made her shiver when she recognised her masked attacker's voice, and she took a deep breath to centre herself as she stood up and paced around the room. "Listen to me carefully. If you don't leave me alone, I'll contact every journalist I know. Tell your bosses that I'll damage them as much as they want to damage me," she said in a calm voice.

There was an abrupt silence on the line before he disconnected it, and Rebecca took a shaky breath as she collapsed suddenly on her chair and leaned her elbows on the table for support. She looked at Leo, relieved that she understood human psychology. "The thug will need to check his orders with Regina before he does anything else," she said.

Leo's eyes widened in concern. "Was that who I think it was? Isn't it dangerous to defy them?"

Rebecca crossed her arms. "I'm not going to be a sitting duck anymore. The delay will buy me some time. If I give in to them, they'll bully me as much as they can, so I need to level the playing field," she said.

Leo snorted. "Surely you don't expect Regina and her husband to give up that easily. They've been on a mission since 1960," he said.

Rebecca's stomach churned, and she wiped away tears with a defiant motion of her hand. Leo's eyes were grave as he said: "Rebecca, we've made the difficult decision to help you. You're right. Regina has gone too far."

Rebecca suppressed more relieved tears. "I know it's a huge decision," she said.

"I'm not sure why we let it go on for so long, we allowed her to get away with far too much," Sam said from the doorway.

Rebecca shook her head, a vehement look on her face. "I've come across several anti-socials in my career. They use intimidation to create an atmosphere of fear. Even psychologists are susceptible to sociopaths, so try not to blame yourselves, that's what Regina wants," she said.

"The entire situation is simply intolerable; we've reached our limit. Without peace of mind, it feels like there's nothing left to lose," Sam said as he joined them at the table.

Leo sipped his whiskey. "There's another problem. Addington protects his organisation at the highest levels. That's how they get away with their crimes, by carrying out a powerful person's agenda," he said.

"What about your source in Reclamation? Can he or she help?" Rebecca said.

Leo avoided her eyes. "I can't tell you who they are, Rebecca. We must protect them. If Regina or Addington discover our source's identity, they'll kill them."

Sam's mobile phone beeped with a text message, and he paled as he read it. "Rebecca, Reclamation is planning to murder you! My source just sent me a message. We must hide you, get you somewhere safe," he said in a tight voice.

Rebecca swallowed her fear and felt calm now that it was time to fight. Her hands clenched into fists. "No. I'm going to the media right now. Sometimes the best place to hide is in plain sight. Don't worry. I'll keep your names out of it," she said.

Sam and Leo looked at each other with raised eyebrows. "Are you sure that's wise? What will you use for proof?" Sam said.

She paused and blew out a sigh through pursed lips. "You're right, that's a problem. It's my word against the Addington's. I need tangible proof," she said.

Leo put his hand on her wrist. "Think this through, Rebecca, are you absolutely sure?" he said.

Rebecca yanked her hand from under his. Her skin felt raw to the touch. "I've thought it through over and over again. When I shine a media spotlight on Regina, Reclamation will have to go back underground. They'll be on the back foot," she said through gritted teeth.

"What about Alex's safety? Are you willing to risk that too?" Sam said, looking into her eyes.

She pushed her chair away from them both and stood up. "Don't worry, I'll leave his name out of it. My only intention is to help Alex. The media are always happy to run a conspiracy theory. I'll focus on Regina and try to get the authorities to track her cronies down."

Leo braced his shoulders. "So, it's come down to the final fight," he said, standing up stiffly and walking to a cupboard where he took out a photograph. "We promised to help you and we'll keep our word. Our undercover source took this photograph," he said, placing it on the table.

Rebecca reluctantly moved back to her chair to look at the photograph next to her wine and brought her hand to her mouth. A blond woman in her 70s dressed in a tight skirt and high heels stood next to Lord Addington. She had narrowed, icy blue eyes starkly outlined with mascara, wrinkles, and dark eyeshadow. Next to her was a younger woman who looked like her daughter. The two women and Addington held guns and flanked a well-dressed government official. All three had the same black tattoo on their arms of an eagle claw clutching a globe.

Rebecca's stomach and shoulder muscles tightened as a shiver ran through her body. "Regina Merin," she whispered. A sheen of cold sweat covered her forehead. Grandmother

Maro's warnings about the evil woman echoed in her mind and she had the sense the past was sucking her into a whirlpool.

"Yes. As you can see, the tattoo on Regina's right arm is Reclamation's symbol," Leo said.

"Is that who I think it is next to her?" she asked when she'd regained her composure.

"Yes, he's in the House of Lords. His name is Terence Salsbury. He's a close friend of Addington's," Leo said.

Rebecca thumped her fist on the table. "So, Reclamation goes all the way to the top. That's what I suspected."

"We think so if Salsbury is involved. And those are just the members we know about," Sam said.

Rebecca picked up the photograph and put it in her bag. "Thank you, Leo. I'll only use it if I must. I know it's a gamble to go to the media, but at least they'll be exposed," she said.

Leo took a deep breath and gently touched her wrist again. "No, use the photograph, Rebecca," he said. "If you give a statement, the photograph will confirm your allegations about the attacker's tattoo and motivation. The police can also trace the phone number he called you from."

This time, Rebecca didn't withdraw her hand and gripped his wrist with her other hand. "Good point. Leo. The photo will help me put Reclamation on the defensive."

Leo squeezed back and then let her hand go. "We've been at their mercy since 1960. It's time to put an end to their reign of terror."

"One more thing, Sam," Rebecca said. "I don't understand how Alex works with the quantum field to produce all these psychic events. You studied physics, do you see any connections?"

Sam's eyes brightened with curiosity and interest. "The brain works with electromagnetic energy and quantum energy," he said. "The right person might consciously control his brain's quantum activity. The results could appear to be parapsychological."

"I recently read an article about Dr. Johnjoe McFadden's idea that consciousness is the brain's energy field. Perhaps consciousness is our brainwaves extending through the quantum field all around us," Rebecca said.

"You must speak more with Sam about that. He could help you connect the dots," Leo said.

Realizing the time, Rebecca grabbed her bag and scarf on the way out of the door. "Good idea, but we must leave it for another time. I'm going to arrange my press conference," she said.

Chapter 10

Her first call was to the foremost journalist in Cyprus, Ioannis Orphanou.

"Ioannis, hi, it's Rebecca."

"Hello, Rebecca, what's up?"

"I have a huge story for you, an exclusive. A thug from a secret British group called Reclamation attacked me to intimidate me into silence," she said.

"What on earth next? Are you okay, Rebecca? Were you badly hurt?" Ioannis said.

"Yes, I'm okay now. Someone stopped my attacker before he could kill me."

"That's crazy. You must call the police, Rebecca. Come to the studio and I'll interview you. I don't understand everything that happened, but it sounds like the public needs to know more about this," Ioannis said.

"I was busy gathering evidence and my next call is to the police. Thank you, Ioannis, I'll be at your studio in a couple of hours."

"Bring your evidence with you for the interview," Ioannis said.

The Nicosia police treated Rebecca's call with the scepticism she'd expected, but they agreed to arrange a meeting with a top-ranking CID detective for later in the day.

Ioannis was an influential media personality who worked for Zeta, a popular and credible television station with a large following. Once he broke the story, the rest of the media would pick it up automatically. That's how the media works, parrot fashion, at least with big news, and Rebecca was banking on the chances her story would get wide coverage. She'd also planned a press conference for the foreign press and newswire agencies. Most of the international media names had offices in Cyprus because it was close enough to cover breaking news in the Middle East, Africa, and Southern Europe.

Once she'd finished the arrangements, Rebecca drove to Zeta TV. She felt nervous and fidgeted with her hands while the crew set up her lighting in the dark room. *Whatever Reclamation plans to do to me, at least the world will know.* She blinked as a crew member switched on the studio lights and Ioannis eased into the interview as they sat opposite each other surrounded by cameras in the spacious studio. The glow of the lights comforted Rebecca after the dark events she'd been through. The floor manager signed '3, 2, 1' and they were live on air.

"Rebecca Vassiliou is a well-known academic and psychologist," Ioannis said to the camera. "Many of you will know her from previous appearances on my show. Today, she's not here to talk about psychology but about a personal attack by a dangerous group called Reclamation. Tell us what happened, Ms Vassiliou," Ioannis said in Greek.

"Thank you, Mr Orphanou. I was about to enter my home when a masked man attacked me from behind and tried to strangle me. I pulled off his mask and saw a symbol tattooed on his neck. Luckily, someone saw I was in trouble and scared off my attacker, but you can still see the bruises on my throat." Rebecca opened her shirt collar as the cameraman zoomed in on the dark blue and red bruises around her neck.

"What did the symbol look like?" Ioannis said.

Rebecca held up a drawing of the eagle's claw clutching a globe. "This is Reclamation's symbol. From my research, they're a British group of wealthy people who want to take control of Cyprus's natural resources because they believe they're entitled to them."

"But surely the time has passed for such anachronistic thinking," Ioannis said.

"We don't live in an ideal world and their psychology is complex," Rebecca said. "They truly believe the mining rights belong to them and that they have a legitimate claim to Cyprus' natural resources. There'd be no reasoning with them because they're too strongly motivated by material gain and a life of entitlement."

"Why did they attack you?"

"I stumbled on them in connection with a paper I'm writing. I didn't know they existed until a few weeks ago."

"So, they're active here in Cyprus?"

"Yes, they've been trying to interfere with the island's future and keep it unbalanced so they can take advantage."

"Other than the attack on you, do you have any proof?" Ioannis said.

Rebecca's hands trembled and she had a sudden awareness of the lights glaring in her eyes. "I have this photograph." She held up the photograph of Regina, which clearly showed a Reclamation tattoo on her arm.

"Who's that?" Ioannis said.

"Her name is Regina Merin, now Lady Addington. Her father was a governor of Cyprus before its independence. She married a wealthy man, wealthy enough to do plenty of damage."

"What have they done to hurt the island's prospects?" Ioannis said.

"Regina and her husband lead a group of mercenaries who are always causing trouble behind the scenes. I know of one incident reported to the police in 1960, just before independence. Reclamation members tried to assassinate President Makarios and the police issued an arrest warrant for Regina Addington."

"Have you contacted the police about this?"

"Yes, we'll meet later today. I've been gathering evidence to take to the authorities," Rebecca said.

Ioannis faced the cameras. "Is Cyprus at risk from this shadowy organisation? Has Dr. Rebecca Vassiliou unmasked a conspiracy to threaten our independence? Our investigative team will take part in uncovering the truth. Until next time, send in your comments as usual," he said, wrapping up the show.

Rebecca's phone rang almost immediately after the studio lights had switched off, leaving the room dim and quiet. It was Sam Carter. "Well done, Rebecca, that's put the cat amongst the pigeons!" he said.

"Thanks, Sam. I'm sure that the interview and exposure will level the playing field. We were fighting at a complete disadvantage until now."

"I've asked a friend to translate your interview into English and send it to her press contacts in the UK," Sam said.

"Good idea. I'll keep the pressure on Regina with a media spotlight."

After the interview, Rebecca headed for police headquarters on the outskirts of Nicosia, praying they'd take her seriously. From an outsider's point of view, it was a tall tale and would be hard to prove but the interview should help her credibility. Word got around quickly in Cyprus judging by the grave look on the face of the senior detective who met Rebecca inside the station.

"Ms. Vassiliou, we're concerned for your safety. Going public has exposed you to more threats. Would you consider witness protection?" the officer said after she gave her statement in an interview room with bare concrete walls.

"Going public was no more dangerous than staying quiet and it depends on what you plan to do about finding the mercenaries," Rebecca said.

"Based on your statement, we've issued local and international arrest warrants for the main suspects," the detective said. "But we don't have anyone else's identity, so we can't guarantee your protection from the other group members. They could be anywhere, and we've no idea how many of them there are."

"The hired gun who threatened me also called me on my mobile phone. Maybe the phone records can help to track him down," Rebecca said.

"We'll get a court order and check the records with the phone company. Do you have a safe place to stay?" the detective said.

"I've no intention of hiding. If you can spare the police officers, I'd be grateful if they would watch my flat. With any luck, they might even catch the goon who threatened me," Rebecca said with more conviction than she felt.

"We work with an independent security company in such cases, so we'll get back to you with an update," the detective said.

"Thank you. Would you like to join my press conference? The international media are waiting outside," Rebecca said.

The detective nodded and said: "The press officer will be there in a minute."

The police headquarters was a simple blue and white building with a massive antenna sticking out of the roof. There were around 15 journalists waiting at the foot of the steps to the building's entrance, each representing one of the global newswires AP, AFP and Reuters.

"I called this press conference because I'm afraid for my life. A secret organisation named Reclamation threatened me

153

to keep me quiet about their plans to destabilise Cyprus so they can take over its natural resources. Do you have questions?" Rebecca said.

"What did the police say, Dr. Vassiliou?" a journalist said.

"They're investigating my allegations. I gave them the evidence I found during my research."

"Why aren't you hiding out in a safe place?" another journalist said.

"I refuse to give in to threats. Their conspiracy goes back a long time and it's reached a new level because they're not afraid to threaten anyone who gets in their way. Someone must stand up to them," Rebecca said.

"Have you spoken to anyone in the Cyprus government?" came another question.

"Not yet. But this organisation is a threat to the government. They're planning something big. I don't know what it is yet. I only know they've hired mercenaries," Rebecca said.

"What about the British government? Are they aware of the danger?" another journalist asked.

"One of their leaders has high-up connections in the British government, but I don't know anything else," Rebecca said.

"Why are they plotting against the government?"

"They want to control the oil and gold here. They're worth billions of Euros," Rebecca said.

"I have a question for the police spokesperson. What measures are you taking to protect Dr. Vassiliou's life and investigate her allegations?" a journalist asked.

"We can't talk about details, but we have prioritised her case at the highest levels," the spokesperson said.

"What do you plan to do next, Dr. Vassiliou?"

"I'm going to get back to my research and try and reach my deadline, I'm sure you all understand," she said with a slight smile. A few of the journalists sent answering smiles and rushed away to get their stories out on the wires.

Just after the press conference, the organizer of the annual psychological symposium, Dr Lognisian, called her from the university where Rebecca worked. "Are you okay? I saw your interview and the news on television," he said.

"Yes, I'm okay for the time being. It was a shock but now that I'm taking action, I feel more in control of the situation," she said.

"I'm sorry to add to the pressure, but I'll need your paper by December 1st so that we can publish it along with the other articles."

"But we agreed on December 31st. The symposium is in the middle of January. There's plenty of time," Rebecca said.

"I know you're under a lot of pressure, but you must hand it in by December 1st or lose your speaking slot. This is your chance to prove that parapsychology exists," Dr Lognisian said.

Never one to turn down a challenge, Rebecca assured him he'd have the work by the new deadline and said her goodbyes. The next call floored her.

"Dr Vassiliou, this is the President's office. President Omeros saw your interview and has asked to meet with you. Can we send a car to pick you up now?" a woman said.

"Yes, of course," she said.

The president's high-powered secret service car arrived, and she got into the back seat, noticing the plush smell of leather. The light inside the vehicle was dim behind windows tinted black for security. Sirens blared their warning wails as the driver sped towards the Presidential Palace.

"We watched your press conference and the interview on Zeta. The secret service has been monitoring Reclamation for some time now and we're on high alert," a man said from the passenger's seat.

"Who are you?" Rebecca said.

"I'm the deputy head of the president's secret service. We've been listening for any information about Reclamation for a few years now. We're trying to find out who really runs it," he said.

Her next question turned into a scream as an on-coming car veered directly into their lane. Time seemed suspended. Rebecca's vision tunnelled. The on-coming vehicle was grey. The paint on the bonnet was peeling and faded. She could just make out the driver's bearish shape as it came towards her in slow motion. A heartbeat later, there was a scraping *crump* as metal crashed into metal with a screech of brakes. Time rushed into the present agonizing moment as the vehicles collided at high speed. The world faded into a dark and dreamless quiet as Rebecca fell into a void

Chapter 11

Rebecca woke up to the astringent, rubbing alcohol smell of a hospital. Marina's classic Cypriot oval-shaped face and concerned eyes were the first things she saw. Her friend's eyes were filled with tears. "Thank God you're awake," Marina said. "I've been so scared waiting for you to come around."

"What's going on? Where am I?" Rebecca mumbled.

Marina patted her shoulder. "You're safe in Eritreon Clinic."

"I…oh my God, what happened?" Rebecca said as a rush of memories came flooding back.

Marina took her hand. "Someone in Reclamation tried to murder you all. The police found the man who was driving the car which hit yours. They said he had one of those tattoos."

"Was it a suicide attack? What happened to the others?"

"The mercenary tried to hit-and-run, but he miscalculated," Marina said. "The police found his body a few meters away from the car. He went straight through the windshield. As for the people in your car - well, the driver is dead."

Tears slid down Rebecca's temple and trickled into her ear. She lifted her right hand to wipe them away and gasped in pain.

"Be careful. You broke your arm in the accident," Marina said, rushing over to help her, bracelets jingling on her arm.

Rebecca's face tightened in pain. "Please Marina, just ask the nurse for a painkiller. I'm in agony."

Marina's eyes creased in concern. "I'm going. You'll be okay, Rebecca, get some rest. I'll turn on the television." She flicked on the TV to distract Rebecca from the pain.

The local channel was broadcasting a presidential press conference and President Omeros was glowering at the camera. "We take attacks on our state very seriously," he said. "The brave woman who exposed the criminal organisation responsible for the attack is in hospital, and one of my guards is dead, along with the car's driver. My condolences to their families. We have already made representations to the British government to investigate this incident."

Marina returned with a nurse who gave Rebecca a painkiller.

"What happened is terrible. These are dangerous people," Marina said when Rebecca was comfortable.

Rebecca's face flushed. "It's all my fault. I caused the media attention. It must have pushed them into this desperate act, what was I thinking?"

"It's not your fault! They're violent criminals who are completely out of control. What were you supposed to do, hide for the rest of your life?" Marina said.

Rebecca couldn't meet her eyes. "No, I don't know, I didn't expect this. I thought the press conference would make them go into hiding, it was a misjudgement."

"Stop blaming yourself. At least the police, the government, and the media on your side now. Before that, you were a sitting duck," Marina said.

A doctor walked into the room. "How are you feeling?" he said.

Rebecca grimaced. "I'm okay. My arm hurts, but otherwise, I feel alright. When can I leave?"

The doctor checked his file. "We're monitoring you for concussion, and I'd prefer you to stay another night," he said. "Your arm needs time to heal, but if you have help from a friend, it shouldn't interfere too much with your life. You're young and will heal quickly."

"I'll be here whenever you need me," Marina said.

Rebecca started crying again. This time she rolled her head to wipe her tears away on the pillow instead of jarring her broken arm, then fell asleep from the exhaustion.

Later, Anastasios woke her up from a deep sleep with anxiety shining from his normally mischievous eyes.

"Anastasios, what are you doing here? How did you know where I was?" Rebecca struggled to her good elbow, but he motioned her to stay put.

"Do you feel well enough to talk about something important?" he said.

"Yes, I can manage."

Anastasios took out an official ID and showed it to her. "I'm sorry about what happened to you, I wish I'd known about your plans, I would have asked you not to hold the press conference. I work in the secret service and the president has assigned me to protect you."

Rebecca peered at the ID. "Assigned you to protect me? You're secret service? What about your bartending job?"

"I work for the president and the bar is a cover, I hear a lot of information when people drink and talk too much. After what happened, the boss asked me to watch over you."

Rebecca was completely taken aback. "I don't know what to say, I had no idea." she said.

Anastasios took her good hand. "I need you to lie low for a few days. Will you do that for me? I can't tell you much else right now."

Rebecca gave him a wry look. "Okay. Not that I have much choice." It was a weak joke, but it lightened the mood and she looked at him with a ghost of a smile. "You're a dark horse, being an undercover agent all this time," she said.

'It wouldn't be much use if everyone knew I was secret service. I'm sorry you've been through the wringer," Anastasios said.

"It's my own fault. I should never have provoked them."

Anastasios looked directly into her eyes. "Try not to blame yourself. You brought them out into the open, the cat-and-mouse games are over, and we'll find out everything now," he said.

Rebecca's expression lightened further. "Thanks. There's another problem. I don't know how to finish my writing with a broken arm."

"After everything you've been through, I'm sure you'll find a way," he said.

"Perhaps, but I'd rather face Regina than Dr. Lognisian, who's determined to have his paper by December 1st."

Anastasios bunched his muscular shoulders to lean in closer to Rebecca. "How far have you reached?"

"I'm about halfway through. I need more information about Alex's mystical abilities," she said.

"What mystical abilities do you mean?"

"About Hzartanek, his higher power."

Anastasios' hand gripped hers and she looked down in surprise. It had felt so natural for his hand to hold hers that she'd forgotten he was still holding it. Anastasios blinked and let go of her hand, pulling back. "Sorry about that. I'm not sure what you mean by Hzartanek."

She smiled at his discomfiture. "I didn't mind. Well, Nick told me about a higher power called Hzartanek. Alex believes he helps him, he's a spiritual guide."

"I didn't know it had a name. We think it's a harmless delusion in the family," Anastasios said with a dismissive twist

162

to his mouth. "Like when a child has an invisible friend. It's a psychological issue. At least, that's what I always thought it was. I could be wrong."

"I'm not so sure. That's what I'm researching. Different sources told me he had a higher power advising him," Rebecca said, starting to feel tired.

Anastasios shrugged. "I can't tell you anything about his so-called mystical abilities. I can tell you other stories about Alex. I remember one that my uncle told me."

Rebecca perked up and nodded with alacrity. "That would be a great help."

"But first, let's talk about how to capture Reclamation's ringleaders," Anastasios said.

"Come a bit closer so we can plan with no one overhearing us," she said. They whispered to each other as their heads moved closer together and although Anastasios didn't take her hand again, she relished the feeling of being next to him.

"Okay, I'll tell you what I know about Alex," Anastasios said out loud after they finished planning their next move.

Rebecca pulled the pale blue blanket over her waist and settled back into the bed to listen as Anastasios leaned back in his chair and stretched his long, muscular legs in front of him. His stories kept her company through the long night.

The next morning, Marina found Anastasios asleep in the chair next to Rebecca, waking them with a start when she closed the door.

"Good morning, sorry to wake you...Anastasios, what are you doing here?" Marina said.

Anastasios stood up, smiled, and kissed her on each cheek.

"It's good to see you, Marina. I haven't seen you in decades."

Rebecca raised an eyebrow. "You two know each other?"

"He's an old family friend, you know Cyprus, everyone's related somehow. I almost didn't recognise him. One of his relatives helped my mother Sophie in the war," Marina said.

Rebecca froze for a moment. "Now wait just a minute. Nick told me a story about how Alexandros hid a woman from the Turkish army, is that who you mean?" she said.

"We must be talking about the same person," Marina answered.

"I need to get back to work. I'll let you two catch up," Anastasios said, touching Rebecca's hand and kissing her lightly on the cheek. The blood rushed to her face as Marina sat next to the bed and winked at her behind Anastasios' back.

"Are you hot? You've gone all red in the face," Marina said as he left.

Rebecca wrinkled her nose at Marina. "Shut up. Thanks for the flowers."

"You're welcome. How do you feel?"

"Enlightened."

Marina smirked. "Why? Is he that good a kisser? He's always had a wicked look in his eyes," she said.

"Stop teasing me, you'll make me laugh and my arm hurts. Did your mother Sophie talk to you about what happened to her during the Turkish invasion?"

Marina rubbed her temple, bracelets jingling. "It was so long ago. My mother ran away from Lefkoniko, our village in the north."

Rebecca took a deep breath. "I need you to find evidence about what happened to your mother during the war," she said.

"So, another mystery?"

"Yes, a mystery that could solve a mystery. I'm looking for independent confirmation of some important information."

Marina leaned forward with an excited glint in her eye. "OK, what type of incident or event am I looking for then?" she said.

"Documents. Look for wartime photographs, a journal, official papers, anything like that," Rebecca said.

"I'll do my best. By the way, one of my students volunteered to help you write your paper. You can dictate it to her," Marina said.

Rebecca smiled. "You're a lifesaver."

The evening painkiller put Rebecca out like a light and her jaw relaxed as she slipped into sleep. A few hours later, she woke up with a start, wincing at the pain in her broken arm. A shadow moved across the sliver of light underneath the door, catching her eye. Someone was outside her room. The door slid

165

open slowly. There was a pain in her ribs and her stomach and chest muscles had cramped from the tension. Light from the corridor haloed around a woman's long, blond hair. Rebecca screamed silently for help and jabbed at the nurse's alert button, but it was just out of reach.

The woman came closer to the bed. Her bony hands stretched out towards Rebecca's neck. Expressionless, wrinkled blue eyes focused on hers. The haggish intruder choked her. There was no air.

Suddenly, Rebecca could gasp for oxygen. The woman's hands fell away from her neck, and she dropped into a black void. Rebecca woke up from the nightmare in tears, her arm throbbing from tossing and turning in her sleep. She checked the sliver of light under the door. It was clear of shadows and anything else, and Rebecca released the trapped breath that was straining her ribs and making her chest ache.

"How did you find out about Reclamation?" a woman said in a stern voice from the corner of the room.

Rebecca's scream ripped out of her mouth. The hospital hush shattered with the noise.

"We can get to you anytime. There's nowhere to hide," the woman said, moving like a shadow away from the bed. The door slid shut behind her dark figure as she left.

Rebecca hadn't seen her face, but she knew it was someone from Reclamation terrorising her. Either Regina had come in person or had sent someone else because she enjoyed tormenting her prey. Rebecca promised herself she'd turn the tables if she ever came face to face with her.

166

A nurse rushed into the room with Anastasios following on her heels.

"Did it work?" Rebecca said.

"Yes, Rebecca, it worked! We caught her red-handed on her way out of the hospital. It was Charlotte Addington, Regina's daughter. She's in handcuffs in the back of a police car," Anastasios said.

Rebecca sighed in relief. "Thank God for that, I wasn't sure if it was Regina or not. She'd risk arrest if she came to our side." Earlier, they'd devised a plan to use her seeming helplessness as bait to trap whoever would come for her from Reclamation.

Anastasios' eyes were warm. "You were right about her arrogance making her reckless," he said.

Rebecca's mouth took on a regretful twist. "I usually use my skills for therapy. Still, at least one of the ringleaders is in custody now."

"How did you know she'd take the bait?" Anastasios said.

"It's their style to bully defenceless people, just look at how Regina treated Alex. She couldn't resist an easy target like me. I didn't anticipate that she'd send her own daughter though," Rebecca said.

Anastasios frowned. "I don't get it. She already has a lot of money and power. She could lose everything by taking such risks."

"Sociopaths can never have enough power; it doesn't occur to them that they might lose." Rebecca smiled at the thought of one plotter safely behind bars, then suppressed the thought. She'd learned that overconfidence was a deadly mistake. There was a long way to go until they defeated the Addingtons and their ambitions.

"How is Charlotte reacting? She must be furious," Rebecca said.

Anastasios raised his chin and tutted in the typical Cypriot way of saying no. "We can't tell. She hasn't said a word."

"What do the secret service and the police think?"

"They're pleased they caught one of them committing a crime. The courts are hard on witness tampering," he said.

Rebecca clenched her fist. "I'll testify that she threatened me."

"Get some rest," Anastasios said on his way to the police station where Charlotte was in custody.

The morning sun woke Rebecca up at 8 am, and the nurse brought her a cup of tea. "You have a visitor; do you feel well enough to meet him?" she said.

"Yes, I feel much better."

Sam Carter walked in, flowers in hand. "Rebecca, how do you feel?" he said.

"I feel like I broke my arm and cracked my head," she said with a rueful smile.

He smiled back and his shoulders relaxed as he arranged the flowers in a blue vase. "I'm glad to see your sense of humour is intact, and you're as spirited as ever."

"Sam, I've been thinking about Alex and his spirit protector. Do you have any insights from the scientific point of view?" Rebecca said.

Sam sat next to her bed. "I grew up with Alex. He used to take care of me when I was little. I always thought he was too good for this world."

Rebecca looked into Sam's eyes. "I have the same feeling when I see him. His soul is pure, he seems to belong in a better place, a utopia."

"I've come to believe that Alex's purity is an energy signal enhancer. It amplifies Hzartanek's energy and intentions to create harmony in the universe," Sam said.

Rebecca raised an eyebrow. "What do you mean?"

"Everything around us vibrates at an energetic frequency. A thought is a vibration, a wave. I believe that Alex can enhance Hzartanek's consciousness to be more powerful. He influences minds and peoples' lives at the quantum level."

"How strong are these thought waves?"

Sam pushed his chair back and paced around the small room. "There have been some recent discoveries but we're still researching how far a brainwave can travel," he said. "Normal brainwaves are weak and don't travel far at the electromagnetic level. Perhaps Hzartanek's energy waves work through the microcosmic field. It's a different story at the quantum level."

"You've lost me," Rebecca said.

Sam held his index fingers far apart.

"At the quantum level, two faraway points can connect. It's called entanglement," he said.

Anastasios walked in and did a double take when he saw Sam. "Hey, man, what are you doing here?" he said.

Sam strode over to Anastasios and gripped his hand. "Brother, it's good to see you. I met Rebecca a few days ago when they attacked her. How's Alexandros? We haven't seen him at the house for a long time."

"I haven't seen him either. He's still in his shell, a recluse," Anastasios said.

"Sam, we've captured your half-sister Charlotte Addington. She was caught threatening me last night," Rebecca said.

"Finally, some good news," Sam said with an intent look in his eyes.

"Did something happen, Anastasios?" Rebecca said.

Anastasios showed them a video of a police interview room. Charlotte's lips were tight, and the dark lines scored on either side of her lips looked like scars. "She's stubborn and refuses to say anything. Do you have any expert advice as a psychologist?" he said.

"Charlotte has had a big shock. Just like her mother, she thought she was invulnerable and cleverer than anyone else," Rebecca said.

Anastasios clacked the phone onto the nightstand. "What do we do then? The police chief told me he has orders to release her. Someone high up is involved," he said, mouth downturned.

Rebecca thought for a moment. "Her mother has twisted her world view. Your best chance is to get her narcissism talking. Let her show off how superior she is to everyone else."

Anastasios looked tired as he crossed his arms. "How do we do that?"

"You need to find a trigger to get her talking," Rebecca said.

"Do you have any suggestions?"

"Are there any English-Cypriot officers in the police force?" she said.

Anastasios snapped his fingers. "I know an English-Cypriot guy called Mike who comes into the bar for a beer every now and then."

"We need someone who looks British and who can speak perfect English," Rebecca said.

"OK, I think he'll do. And what comes next?"

Rebecca narrowed her eyes. "Mike must convince her he's on her side against the Cypriot police. It's risky, but what he needs to do is appeal to her sense of supremacy over others," she said.

Sam's eyebrows knitted. "What are the chances of this working? Charlotte's aggressive, not stupid, won't she see through it?" he said.

"She's still inexperienced, and she looks desperate to me. See the tension lines around her mouth? She might make another mistake. Tell Mike to agree with everything she says and play good cop no matter what comes out of her mouth," Rebecca said.

Anastasios ran out the door with an apologetic look over his shoulder. "I have to work fast before they release her," he said.

Later that day, Marina walked in holding a small trunk in her arms. "I might have found the evidence you're looking for," she said.

Rebecca rubbed her bleary eyes with her good hand as Marina took out a photograph and handed it to her. Rebecca gripped the side of the bed with her good hand. "That's Alexandros standing next to your mother in the hospital. Who took this photograph?" she said.

"Is it? I've never met him. My uncle took the photo just after the '74 war," Marina said. "There's more ancient history in the trunk that she left me, I never got round to looking at it. Her diary's in the box too, I brought it for you to read. What exactly are you looking for?"

"I'll know it when I see it. I'm looking for proof that Alex is a charismatic. I need some solid facts that connect his abilities with parapsychology," Rebecca said.

"He wouldn't be the first psychic in Cyprus," Marina said.

Rebecca nodded. "Exactly. I remember interviewing Marlena Economou, the medium who claimed to channel spirits through her camera. She even showed me how it works. They looked like transparent orbs floating against a black wall," she said.

Marina raised her eyebrows. "Really?"

"Yes. It was hard not to believe her. During the day, she was a research biologist and worked in a lab, she has a lot of integrity as a scientist and isn't one to make things up," Rebecca said.

"Even rational people have their quirks, though," Marina said.

Rebecca shot her an irritated look. "I'm talking about much more than a quirk. I've seen a psychic turn on the radio with his mind and communicate with spirits. Another one shattered a mirror when he focused the energy of his mind onto it," she said.

Marina made a calming motion. "Okay, okay, I didn't mean to upset you. I know how important it is for you to prove that parapsychology exists."

Rebecca clicked her fingertips on the nightstand. "It's a tiny island with a disproportional number of psychics, mystics and saints. How can you explain these phenomena?"

"Seems even stranger when you put it like that," Marina said.

The phone buzzed, breaking their concentration on the puzzles of the paranormal.

"Rebecca, I'm going to Skype you and patch the call through to the live feed of Charlotte's interview," Anastasios said. "We're using your idea of tricking Charlotte with a double agent. I want you to observe the interview and give me your take on what we should do next."

A few minutes later, her Skype app played the familiar blooping ringtone. The tiny telephone screen showed Charlotte sitting at a steel and plastic table in a police interview room surrounded by unpainted concrete walls. She had pulled her hair tightly back from her forehead. In the stark light, her skin was blue-white with dark lines on either side of her mouth and a sharp crease of anger between her eyebrows that deepened when she narrowed her baleful eyes into slits and glared at the two detectives sitting opposite her.

Charlotte slammed her handcuffed wrists on the table. "Your lives won't be worth living if you don't let me out of here. Don't you know who my family is? My father could buy all of you with his pocket change," she snarled.

"Antonis, she's right, we can't keep her here, not after what the High Commissioner said. She's an important British subject. We must release her, otherwise we might lose our jobs," one officer said.

Antonis sneered. "Shut up with that British stuff, Mike. That woman is a criminal, and she's in Cyprus, not Britain. She'll do as she's told. She's not above the law."

"How dare you!" Charlotte hissed.

"Yes, it's over. Get used to it," Antonis said. "We beat the British and kicked you out, so you'll sit there until I say otherwise! Mike, I'm going to get a coffee. See if you can get her to tell us why she tried to intimidate the psychologist. Was she trying to kill her again?" Antonis left the holding room.

Charlotte glared at Mike, who moved closer to her and murmured: "The High Commissioner wants you released."

She swayed her head closer to Mike's and focused on his eyes like a cobra. "So, what am I still doing in this stinking room?" she whispered.

"To tell you the truth, you should know that the guy who just left was a member of EOKA."

"Those worthless terrorists. No wonder they're treating me like this," Charlotte said.

"But I don't feel the same about you. I'm half-English. The good half," Mike said.

"Half good's better than all bad," Charlotte said with a rictus smile.

"Look, I want to help you. I admire you," Mike said. "I hate what EOKA did to Cyprus and to the British army. They disgust me and I agree with you that they're terrorists. From the moment I heard about your organisation on TV, I wanted to be a member. I belong with you," Mike said.

Over in the hospital, Rebecca and Marina watched Charlotte's face closely. Would she suspect a trick or fall for the flattery? Charlotte looked down at the table as a small smile played around her lips.

"We've got her, hook, line and sinker," Rebecca said.

Marina nodded. "It's incredible how arrogant psychopaths are. Flattery works every time." Both

175

psychologists focused on the drama playing out on the small screen of Rebecca's mobile phone.

Charlotte took her time before she answered Mike. "What do I have to do to get out of here?" she said. "My mother's powerful. Her organisation could help your career beyond your wildest dreams. We have people with real power behind us. It's difficult to become a member of Reclamation, but I could persuade my parents if you help me. There's plenty of money in it for you."

"I'll help you to escape. Follow my lead," Mike said. He uncuffed her hands and grabbed her elbow as the pair left the interrogation room.

Marina and Rebecca looked at the empty interview room on the tiny phone screen, and then at each other. "I hope he knows what he's doing. It's a dangerous game he's playing," Marina said.

Rebecca called Anastasios. "She fell for our plan, but your agent is going to have to be careful. Are you in touch with him? He's in danger," she said.

"Yes, we have eyes on him constantly. There are seven agents following them. Do you have any other advice, Rebecca?" he said.

"Try and meet with Sam Carter. He has a source in Reclamation, someone who feeds him information. He wouldn't tell me their name, but he might give you the identity if you ask him," Rebecca said.

"Okay, I'll get on it. Anything else about Charlotte's state of mind?" Anastasios said.

"It's not about Charlotte at this point, it's about her parents. They'll feel like they won a victory and might get even more cocky now that she's escaped. This time, they'll make a real mistake," Rebecca said.

"What kind of mistake?"

"Regina and Addington are single-minded and vindictive and I'm getting in their way. I think they'll come back to finish me," Rebecca said.

Anastasios drew in a sharp breath. "I have undercover police watching your hospital room."

"They'll be expecting that. The alternative is that they'll organise a political assassination to gain more power," Rebecca said. "Maybe against the president or another high-up political figure. An assassination would destabilise the country, which is what they want. It'd be easy for them to get rid of me after that."

"The Secret Service is already on high alert and protecting the president," Anastasios said.

"Charlotte believes the British High Commissioner is on her side. She'll tell her parents and they might try to contact him as a sympathiser."

"We'll alert his secret service now," Anastasios said before hanging up.

Marina handed Rebecca her mother's battered leather-bound journal and left. The hours wore on and Rebecca almost wished Regina would show up to relieve the boredom. She had just drifted off to sleep when the doctor woke her up at around 9:00 pm.

"Sorry to wake you, Rebecca but we've been asked to move you to another room," he said.

Rebecca groaned inwardly. She realised the move was to keep her safe, but it was painful and for the first time, she understood how difficult it would be to manage life with a broken arm. She set her jaw, knowing that the answer didn't lie in feeling weak, and tried to distract herself from the pain in her arm by deep breathing.

Once in her new room, Rebecca calmed down. All around her, the night whispered and murmured its dark song. She heard the nurse's soft, rhythmic footsteps, the clink of glasses on a nightstand, the wind susurrating through the giant eucalyptus trees in the hospital gardens. For a moment, she felt at peace and the cramped ball of anxiety in the pit of her stomach eased.

Rebecca picked up the diary Marina had left for her to read. A quick scan of the contents confirmed that Alex had saved Sophie's life by taking her to the hospital when she gave birth. Sophie wrote that it was a miracle that Alex had found food for her family all through the worst of the fighting. In the entry for September 3, 1974, she reminisced about Alex and his friend Hzartanek. Rebecca gripped the diary, and her heart pounded when she read the name of Alex's spirit protector.

'I think he must be Russian. Such a name – Hzartanek,' Sophie had written. 'He helped Alex to find us food and water so we could survive the war. Hzartanek guided Alex through the fighting to safety, at least that's what he told me. I've never seen him personally. Alex has been so kind to us. We would never have made it through the war without his help.'

178

Rebecca put the diary down, deep in thought about how she would present Hzartanek in her paper. She looked up and gasped at the sound of the door handle clicking open and the sight of a gaunt silhouette at the entrance to the room. It was the last person she'd expected to see. "Alexandros! What on earth are you doing here?"

Alex walked into the room, holding a warning forefinger against his lips. He switched off the light and signalled for her to stay still before crouching behind the bed. Rebecca heard another click as the door handle turned. A woman entered the room. The light from the corridor reflected on white-blond hair. Regina walked towards the bed. She must have had an informer in the hospital to know that Rebecca had switched rooms. The security guards were useless. They were guarding the wrong room.

Alex flung his arms up over his head, and the intruder cringed back towards the door. He gaped open his mouth at her silently, like Munch's painting 'The Scream'. Regina stood still as a statue and stared at him as a white substance poured out of Alex's mouth, and his body arched into a rigid C curve.

Rebecca blinked hard, but the white cloud was still there when she opened her eyes. It enveloped them so thickly that she could barely see. Then, everything went as black and quiet as the deepest, darkest of sleeps.

Chapter 12

Rebecca woke up feeling nauseous 30 minutes later and glanced around the hospital room. Alex had vanished along with the white cloud and Regina was lying motionless on the floor in the corner next to the door. Rebecca's hands shook on her mobile phone as she called Anastasios and whispered: "Regina's knocked out cold and she might wake up any minute."

"Where are the undercover agents, how did she get past them?" Anastasios said.

"The doctor moved me to another room, so the agents were waiting for Regina in my old room."

"Then how the hell did she know where you were? I made sure your room was under tight security."

"I don't know who told her. Maybe she paid off one of the hospital staff, bribery's her style," Rebecca said.

"I'll call the agents now," Anastasios said as hung up.

A few minutes later, three men in plain blue jeans and black t-shirts walked into Rebecca's room and handcuffed Regina. "What happened to her?" one of them said.

"I need to speak with Anastasios first," Rebecca said, wincing as she rubbed her sore arm.

"He's on his way, hang in there."

A nurse lifted the unconscious Regina onto a wheeled hospital bed.

"Where are you taking her?" Rebecca said.

"The boss told us to take her to a secure part of the hospital for examination, and then we'll see. Anastasios will keep you updated," the agent answered.

Rebecca reached for her phone again and winced as the nerves in her broken arm burned. Anastasios rushed through the doorway and knelt by her bedside. "Are you ok? What happened, Rebecca?" he said, his eyes locking with hers.

Tears pricked Rebecca's eyes. "I'm alright. Alex was here. A white cloud came out of his mouth and then I lost consciousness," she said.

"It's hard to believe that a cloud of… whatever it was, came out of him. But if I believe that, then what did Alex do to Regina? Why is she in a coma and you're not?"

"We can only find out by talking to her when she wakes up. If she wakes up," Rebecca said.

The doctor released her later that day and Anastasios gave her a lift home. Once he'd checked the flat for any intruders, he settled her on the couch and switched on the TV.

"Have you talked with Mike? Is he still undercover?" Rebecca said.

"No, he went home. That reminds me, he said he had some information to tell me," Anastasios said.

Rebecca touched his forearm. "Do you know what it is? He might have crucial information about Regina's accomplices."

Anastasios shook his head. "I asked him to meet us here so he can tell us himself."

Mike rang Rebecca's doorbell 20 minutes later and Anastasios let him in. "Have a seat. This is Rebecca, the psychologist I told you about who's helping us. What can I bring you to drink, Mike?" Anastasios said.

Mike's jaw jutted forward. He was stocky and looked like he meant business. "I'll have a whiskey, neat, thanks," he said.

He sat next to Rebecca in the living room and sipped the whiskey Anastasios had brought him. Rebecca lurched up on her good elbow into a sitting position. "Mike, what did you find out?" she asked.

Mike scanned the room slowly, taking in the light green walls and comfortable, dark red furniture. He ran his gaze over the bookshelves and took a deep breath before glancing at Anastasios, eyebrows raised.

"It's okay, you can trust her," Anastasios said.

"We went to a mansion just outside Nicosia in Dali village. That's where they're all hiding out," Mike said.

"Other than Charlotte, who was there?" Rebecca asked.

Mike's lips tightened. "I counted around 20 other people. Regina and her husband were there with a bunch of mercenaries who were all just as frightening as she is."

"She's hiding in plain sight. Did you know there's still an arrest warrant for Regina on our side? What's their plan?" Rebecca said.

"They mostly talked about the profits they'd make from mining." Mike took a long sip of his drink. "I've seen a lot of things as an undercover cop, but they really gave me the creeps," he said.

"Did you hear any details about their plans?" Anastasios said.

"They gave away a few details about taking control over the mining rights," Mike said.

Rebecca blew out a frustrated breath through pursed lips. "So, you heard nothing that could give us a clue about what they're planning?"

"Not directly. I've got someone on the inside, though," Mike said. "The cook's a distant relative of mine. She's not happy that they treat her like a slave. She's promised to call me if she hears anything we can use to catch them in the act," Mike said.

"Were you in any danger?" Anastasios said.

"I don't think so, I played it safe. They liked it when I told them that the British High Commissioner sympathises with them."

Anastasios and Rebecca exchanged a look.

"Maybe we can use this. Call your relative and ask her what's going on, please," Anastasios said.

Mike left the room to talk to his source and when he came back, his face was white, shoulders bunched high against his neck. Anastasios gripped his arm. "Mike, what's wrong?" he said.

"There are more men at the mansion. My relative told me she recognised one of them, a fanatical militant right-winger, someone high-up in the Turkish government," Mike said through gritted teeth.

"Jesus!" Anastasios said.

"Is she sure?" Rebecca said.

Mike nodded. "Yes, she recognised him before they told her to leave the house."

"How did he cross to our side?" Anastasios said.

Mike scoffed. "It's easy to cross over from the occupied areas, there are many ways," he said.

Anastasios punched in a number on his mobile phone. "I have to call my boss, this is not good," he said.

"Maybe he's next-in-command in their organisation. They had to bring him in now that Regina's in a coma," Rebecca said.

Mike raised an eyebrow. "In a coma?"

Rebecca nodded. "Yes, she was captured last night after another attempt on my life in the hospital," she said.

A movement on the TV caught Rebecca's eye and she saw tanks rolling up the avenue leading to the Presidential Palace. "What the hell is going on? Something's happening. Anastasios, look!"

A reporter appeared on the screen, keeping a wary eye over his shoulder. "Happening now. The National Guard is surrounding the Presidential Palace to defend President Omeros after information that a coup is imminent," he said.

Mike and Anastasios' footsteps pounded as they ran out of the front door. "Please stay here, Rebecca, don't leave the flat until I tell you it's safe. Take care of your arm," Anastasios said over his shoulder.

Rebecca grimaced as grinding pain throbbed in her arm and she propped the limb up on a pillow as she watched TV. The situation unravelled quickly. The reporter ducked as gunshots barked out somewhere off camera and the tanks kept rumbling towards the Presidential Palace, lumbering up to the entrance and turning to face the gated road leading up to the symbolic building. Two platoons of National Guard soldiers ran to reinforce the gate that led up to the wooded hill in front of the Presidential Palace. More shooting came from somewhere off-camera. The soldiers took cover and returned fire.

Rebecca's eyes widened when she saw the Light Walker standing directly in front of the tanks. A blaze of light was streaming from his body in all directions, and the soldiers backed away in awe. The shooting stopped, and the screen went black as the camera stopped transmitting to the station.

After the shock, Rebecca fell asleep from utter exhaustion. A noise from the television woke her up at 3 am and she ached from head to toe, her arm throbbing as she held it to her chest.

WAR!

The word scrolled endlessly across the television screen, and it took several minutes for her to understand what the reporter was saying.

"The National Guard is defending the Presidential Palace for the moment, but the situation is precarious," the journalist said as he furrowed his forehead and glanced around the area, searching for any new threats. "From what we know so far, Turkey is trying to annex the rest of Cyprus with a coup instigated by a paramilitary group named Reclamation. Hasan Küçük is waiting in the wings to take over from our president, who's in imminent danger of assassination."

The images on the screen blurred and Rebecca blinked away the tears from her eyes. She couldn't believe her country was once again back at war. The footage of Alex standing in front of the tanks reappeared on the screen and the reporter gasped in a breath, focusing his gaze on the eye of the camera. "Everyone is asking about the extraordinary man you see on your screen who delayed the enemy long enough for the Greek army to reach the Presidential Palace and hold off the coup," he said.

Rebecca waited for the bright flash of white light around Alex, but the station cut the footage short and looped back to the beginning of the shot when Alex had walked into the frame. They must have thought the blazing light that Alex had emitted was a technical glitch. But by now, she knew better, it was obvious that Hzartanek was at work again, sending waves of cosmic energy to rebalance the forces of war and violence.

The sound of the phone ringing surprised Rebecca and when she checked the screen, Marina's name appeared on it. "Are you okay, my friend?" Marina said. "We're all staying home because of the war, but I'm thinking about you. Do you need anything? I could risk coming over."

Rebecca squeezed her eyes shut, frustrated that she couldn't seem to stop tearing up. "No, don't risk it. I'm okay," she said.

"What do you think is going to happen?" Marina said.

"I'm not sure, but it looks bad. Did you see Alex in front of the tanks?"

"My God, yes, it was incredible to watch, he was so brave. I heard the Greek army is protecting him now," Marina said.

Rebecca's call waiting buzzed. "Marina, I'll call you back. It's Anastasios, I must get this." She could barely hear Anastasios's voice, and her gut clenched. "Are you okay?" she said.

Anastasios's voice grew louder. "Yes, I'm just exhausted. The situation is completely out of control."

"Where are you?"

"I'm at the Presidential Palace, guarding the president. Are you watching the news? Will anyone help Cyprus?"

Rebecca checked the headlines on her TV screen. 'GREECE, USA send reinforcements to Cyprus to counter Turkey's attack. FRANCE WILL DEFEND Cyprus - President Rousseau."

Rebecca's voice was tight as she read the headlines out loud. "Anastasios, they're sending reinforcements from Greece and the USA. How long can you hold out?"

"We've seen at least three hundred enemy Reclamation militants. They're softening up the target ahead of another invasion by Turkey. They must have been hiding in the north," Anastasios said.

"How's the president?"

"He's holding up well. The British High Commissioner is at the Palace, they're thinking about mediating with Reclamation."

Rebecca gripped the phone. "Is the UK government behind Reclamation's attack, or are they acting on their own?"

"We're still not sure, Rebecca. Prime Minister Harlow made a statement to support Cyprus, so Reclamation doesn't have any official sanction from the top."

"Still, there must be powerful people high up in the UK government who are helping them," Rebecca said. "People who connected them with Turkey and gave them enough money and resources to start a war."

Anastasios's voice faded again. "Fanatics always find powerful backers. We just don't know who they are, other than Addington."

"Do you think there could be an internal split in the British government?" Rebecca said.

Anastasios' voice dropped again. "Anything's possible right now. The world has gone crazy. All I can do is protect the President."

"How can I help?"

"Just stay safe, Rebecca. I need to know you'll be careful. Once this is over, we'll be able to think more clearly."

The line disconnected, and she looked at the television, hoping in vain that Anastasios would appear on the screen.

"We're switching to a live feed at the Presidential Palace, and I'll be back with more updates," the news anchor said.

National Guard tank reinforcements had manoeuvred into place to protect the president. It was going to take more than 300 militants to break through unless more troops come from Turkey or north Cyprus. Just as the thought crossed her mind, Rebecca saw more tanks rolling up the avenue that led to the Presidential Palace. The red Turkish flag glared at her from the screen, and she realised there was going to be a stand-off. Five Turkish tanks took up their positions facing the seven National Guard tanks. They must have crossed through the Green Line just a few kilometres away.

Time froze for a long moment.

The thump and crash of tanks firing directly at each other shattered the silence into a thousand percussive, jagged pieces. Rebecca swallowed, fighting the nausea souring her mouth as her heart pounded, and she breathed deeply to calm down. The war played out surreally on television like a movie and she had to force herself to believe it was real.

A National Guard tank slowly tipped over on its side from the force of an explosion from a Turkish anti-tank missile. Black smoke covered the tank and soldiers scrambled to escape out of the hatch. Several of them stumbled and fell in their flight from the death trap as gunfire crackled all around them. A National Guard attack helicopter swooped down and the crew opened fire on the Turkish tanks to cover the National Guard soldiers, who ran to take shelter behind the walls of the Presidential Palace.

Rebecca's phone rang almost as loudly as her jangled nerves, and she realised she'd forgotten to call Marina back, but the name which popped up on her screen wasn't the one she was expecting. It was Sam Carter. "Rebecca, I'm calling to see if you're all right. How's your arm?" he said.

"It's still the same. I'm watching the battle outside the Presidential Palace. It's terrifying. How are you? Are Willow and Leo with you?"

"Yes, they're here. We're all okay," Sam said. "Our source in Reclamation sent me a video of a meeting between Regina and the other ringleaders. I have it all on record, their names and what they plan to do once Cyprus is under their control."

Rebecca's stomach lurched again. "Can you send it to me by email?" she said. "It's urgent to inform the Secret Service right now, the information might mean the difference between war and peace. Anastasios is with the president and if they watch it together, it could make all the difference."

"I'm sending it through now," Sam said before he hung up.

More frightening headlines scrolled relentlessly across the screen.

EUROPE AND THE USA ARE UNITED IN DEFENDING CYPRUS FROM TURKEY....

TURKISH TROOPS GATHER ALONG THE GREEN LINE... FURTHER INVASION OF CYPRUS IS IMMINENT!

Another news anchor appeared, her face pale under a harsh studio spotlight. "We interrupt our live feed outside the Presidential Palace with an urgent update," she said. "Europe and the USA have issued a joint statement against Turkey and plan to cancel the country's NATO membership. The world powers say their navy and air forces have signed an emergency joint agreement to protect Cyprus. The UK has warned Turkey to withdraw its troops completely from the island before it triggers World War III."

Footage of Turkey's leader Erdogan in front of a microphone flashed onto the screen. "Cyprus is ours, it belongs to the motherland!" he trumpeted.

"Turkey is defiant. Erdogan has issued a statement saying that the UK and Turkey had agreed that Cyprus would come under their joint control as guarantors," said the anchor. "But the UK denied the alliance. The conflict has divided NATO forces and world leaders are scrambling to find solutions. Greece has already sent its navy and air force to Cyprus and we expect them within a few hours."

"God save me from this insanity. The Addingtons have a lot to answer for," Rebecca muttered as her computer bleeped an email notification, interrupting the bad news on the television. It was the email she'd been expecting from Sam. Rebecca downloaded the video and hit play. The timestamp was a few days earlier, just before the attempt on her life.

In the video, Regina and Lord Addington sat at a table with three more people. Two of them were well-known members of the House of Lords; Terence Salsbury, and Defence Minister Sharon Ripley. Rebecca didn't recognize the third man. Perhaps he was Sam's source. Whoever had filmed it had hidden the video in a bag and a flap of material partly obscured the scene. Regina's eyes narrowed as she glared at Ripley. "The time to act is now, we've been planning for long enough. Our Turkish allies want to move against Cyprus immediately," she hissed.

Sharon Ripley stood up and slammed her hands on the table. "Don't be absurd, Regina, it's far too early. We must do the groundwork first. You don't know the first thing about military ops," she said.

"Give me my money first, and then I'll back your bill, Regina," Terence Salsbury said.

Regina sneered and pushed a suitcase over the table towards her treasonous accomplices. "The first three million pounds are in the case. You'll get the rest after I'm satisfied you've finished the job," she said. "Prepare the Reclamation Bill and push it through Parliament. Make sure it says our national security is the top priority and that ex-colonies like Cyprus are a security risk because they support terrorism against the United Kingdom. Once the House passes the bill, we'll do the rest."

"What about the possibility of a war with Greece? The Greeks guarantee Cyprus' security," Ripley said.

"The Turks will deal with them. They're our strongest allies in the Eastern Mediterranean," Regina said.

"What will happen to the British army bases on Cyprus?" Ripley said.

"Are you dense? I told you; we need the UK troops in Cyprus to help Turkey when it attacks the Presidential Palace and replaces the president with our Turkish man," Regina said.

"That won't happen without the prime minister's approval," Salsbury said.

"Then get it. That's what I paid you to do!" Regina snapped.

Salsbury smiled, but his eyes narrowed. "Now, now, Regina, don't be unreasonable. Short of kidnapping the man or blackmailing him, I don't know what else to do. The Prime Minister's a passionate believer in Cyprus's independence. He won't support your plan," he said.

Suddenly, the video went blank and Rebecca held her head in her hands, feeling dizzy. Then she inhaled deeply, suddenly realising she'd held her breath for too long. Here was indisputable proof that treacherous, high-up British officials were plotting against Cyprus. She had to get the evidence to the British Prime Minister through the High Commissioner who was sheltering in the Presidential Palace with the president, surrounded by tanks and militants. She could only do that through Anastasios.

The video restarted suddenly, jarring Rebecca's nerves.

"Walk me through the plan," Ripley said.

"Once the House approves the Reclamation Bill, we'll pull the trigger on a false flag Greek-Cypriot terrorist attack on the UK. Turkey will step in to take over the government and put one of its own in power. Our Turkish allies have agreed to have a British vice-president," Regina said.

"You'll never get the Cypriots to vote for a Turkish president and a British vice-president. That's a fool's plan," Salsbury murmured.

"Who cares about votes? We're planning a military coup. It's your problem to control the population, not mine," Regina spat. "Your spooks know how to manipulate public opinion. It can be a dictatorship for all I care. What we want is total control over Cyprus' mining rights."

"So you keep saying, but if we don't get legal cover from the Reclamation Bill, the government won't support military action in Cyprus," Ripley said.

Rebecca paused the video to think. Regina hadn't had the time to push her poisonous bill through to a vote. They had no legal cover, no matter how thin. That must be why Turkey was hesitating, massing troops instead of attacking fully. Her press conference had forced their hand and disrupted their plans. She called Anastasios, who answered after 20 long rings.

"What is it, Rebecca? I'm about to go into the Presidential Palace," he said.

"Anastasios, this is important. I'm sending you a video. Show it to the president and High Commissioner," Rebecca said. "It's solid proof of all the treacherous people who are plotting with Regina. If you act quickly, the president has enough leverage to demand that England end the war before it begins and destroys us all."

Anastasios's voice lifted with hope. "Send it to me. I'll show it to the boss as soon as I get it," he said.

Rebecca hit the send button.

At the Presidential Palace just a few miles away, Anastasios carried his laptop into the war conference room and set it on the President's desk. As they watched the video of Regina plotting the end of Cyprus's independence, the president's shoulders slumped.

"What are we going to do, Your Excellency?" the president said, turning to the High Commissioner. "Give me some answers to stop this war. These are British citizens trying to destroy my country and they've brought the Turkish army to my front gates!"

"The best thing we can do is to send this video to my Prime Minister. He'll know how to handle it," the High Commissioner said.

"Get him on the phone. He must see this immediately," the president said.

Anastasios left the politicians to it and went outside to check the situation with the Turkish tanks. He could clearly see the stand-off from the top of the hill, and it didn't look good. More tanks had joined the first five and he estimated there were around 12 enemy tanks now, sitting silent and menacing. Out of the corner of his eye, he spotted more tanks moving in. The latest arrivals carried the blue and white flag of Cyprus' ally, Greece. Anastasios glanced down at his mobile phone to check that the news was still broadcasting because this would mean the enemy had not yet struck at the communications infrastructure.

Now that he'd seen the conspirators' video, Anastasios understood that the invasion and attempted coup were on the spur of the moment. There was still a chance to defend and oust the invaders if the Allies joined Cyprus and Greece's efforts. So far, the Allies had shown outspoken support for Cyprus, which was a European Union border and with Regina in a coma, her plans were weakened. "Thank God for small mercies," Anastasios muttered.

Headlines scrolled across the screen of his mobile phone. French naval reinforcements had joined the US warships guarding Cyprus' coastline and preventing the Turkish navy from entering Limassol and Famagusta ports. French and Israeli jets were circling the island's airspace, blocking the Turkish air force from covering its ground troops and tanks.

The Greek defence minister appeared on TV, underdressed in jeans and a t-shirt. He must have been out with friends when the emergency hit the Greek news channels. "I speak for the entire European Union when I say that Greece will not tolerate Turkey's actions in Cyprus," he said. "We demand a full withdrawal from the island and immediate reparations for the damages caused by yet another brutal invasion. The US has joined the European Union to defend the

196

island and the sooner that Turkey leaves Cyprus, the better it will be for them."

Another headline scrolled across the screen: EU LEADERS SUMMARILY END TURKEY'S MEMBERSHIP BID...

SANCTIONS IMPOSED ON ERDOGAN, TURKISH GOVERNMENT...

TRADE WITH TURKEY SUSPENDED...

EU-US JOINT OPERATION FACES DOWN TURKISH MILITARY.

The Allies had surrounded the 40,000 Turkish troops in Cyprus with an overwhelming force. Short of going to a full-out war with NATO, Ankara had no choice but to retreat, but to Anastasios's confusion, Turkey's troops hadn't yet turned tail and withdrawn from their vulnerable position. The Turkish leader, Erdogan, appeared determined to bluff it out, no matter what the cost.

A heavy explosive thump made Anastasios snap his head up in alarm. A Turkish tank had fired on the hill, aiming at the thick mini forest that camouflaged the Presidential Palace. Immediately, the Greek and Cypriot tanks returned fire to the enemy, bombarding it with heavy munitions and the Turkish tank went silent. A Secret Service agent ran out of the Presidential Palace as cracks appeared in the sandstone masonry.

"Anastasios! What's happening? The ground is shaking so much that the President lost his balance," he said in a trembling voice.

The muscles in Anastasios' throat were rigid and his shoulders were boxed. "A Turkish tank tried to bombard the Presidential Palace; they're going all the way," he said.

"My God, they're too close. We must get the president somewhere safe."

"What's he doing now?" Anastasios said.

"He's speaking with the British Prime Minister. Omeros asked him to take the culprits into custody and join the fight against Turkey."

Anastasios gripped the other agent's shoulder. "Things are getting worse. Turkey will annihilate us if Erdogan invades with his full military force."

"It's time to take the president to the secure bunker and then transport him out of the country," the other agent said. Anastasios followed him back into the Presidential Palace. After fifteen minutes of wrangling, the President agreed to leave with his security guard and the British High Commissioner. The group of men strode to a low-profile sedan car so common on the road it was almost invisible. As they bundled into the car, another explosive thump shook the ground. The driver headed to an electric gateway, which opened and closed behind the vehicle. He switched off the ignition as the men heard the click and whir of a machine and the ground lowered slowly beneath them.

When the hidden elevator stopped, the car was 20 meters underground facing a dark tunnel. The driver switched on the ignition and the headlights as he sped through the tunnel for half an hour. They emerged into a dawning day, close to

Larnaca, heading for a secret airbase. Once they'd reached the airbase, the President and High Commissioner boarded a helicopter en route to Greece. Relieved, Anastasios drove back to Nicosia, listening to the news on the radio.

"We've just confirmed that an Israeli warplane shot down a Turkish F16 flying along the Famagusta coastline," the newsreader said.

Anastasios whistled in admiration. The Israelis didn't mess around.

"Two more US aircraft carriers have arrived off the coast of Limassol. Meanwhile, US President Shore reiterated his call to Turkey to withdraw all troops immediately from Cyprus," the newsreader said.

Anastasios switched off the radio and called an agent in his unit. "Petros, what's happening at the Palace?" he said.

"We just heard that tank reinforcements from Greece are on the way. The US navy is escorting them over. The Turkish tanks haven't fired since the second bombardment. It's a stand-off," Petros said.

"I'm on my way back, hold tight." Anastasios floored the accelerator.

Chapter 13

It was a mystery why Turkey held off on a full attack. Was it waiting for its ally, the UK, to get the Americans on their side and complete their invasion? The enemy didn't know that the president was no longer in Cyprus and maintained a siege and standoff against Greek and Cypriot troops outside the Presidential Palace. Then, Turkey issued a 24-hour ultimatum. Either the President surrendered the state to Ankara's control or there'd be a full-scale war.

Events moved quickly after Turkey's declaration, events that television stations were to broadcast worldwide. American warships confronted Turkey's army off the coast of Cyprus and blockaded them from entering the island's waters. The Israeli air force attacked every Turkish warplane trying to enter the island's airspace, backed by France's naval and air power. A million civilians sheltered at home, praying for a quick resolution.

After some delay, the UK's Prime Minister expressly refused to support Turkey and denied being part of Reclamation's plot. The authorities arrested Sharon Ripley and more ringleaders in London, leaving Turkey isolated, surrounded by NATO forces, and abandoned by its allies. A few days later, Turkey gave in to the immense pressure and unexpectedly withdrew all troops from Cyprus, leaving a stunned population in its wake. The Turkish-Cypriot leadership quickly started high-level meetings with the government, which appeared to be going well.

After Turkey's withdrawal from Cyprus, Rebecca felt safe enough to take a walk to the *Safe Haven* bar and have a drink with Anastasios. His eyes lit up when she walked into the busy bar, and he greeted her with a warm hug, careful to avoid hurting her broken arm. She snuggled him back, luxuriating in the warm, spice-violet smell of his neck. Her muscles relaxed, and she realised how tense she'd been.

"How's your paper going, Rebecca?"

"It's going well," Rebecca said. "Marina found me a student intern who's helping me a lot with transcribing my work, so I'll be able to hand it in before the deadline. I sent the synopsis to the symposium's organiser, and he said it looks brilliant."

"That's great! What did you decide about the title?"

"It's called Empath to Mystic - Proving the Existence of Parapsychology."

"Congratulations," Anastasios said, giving her another hug.

"Thanks, it's just the beginning. I'm sure that all the sceptics can't wait to debunk my work," Rebecca said. "I'm getting ready for a big debate."

They smiled at each other, and Rebecca felt her face go as red as her wine. After experiencing so much together, spending time with him felt familiar and exciting at the same time and she savoured the moment. When she looked up, his eyes locked with hers. "Do you want to have dinner with me tomorrow night?" he said.

"Yes, I'd love to," she answered, wondering why the sounds of the bar had faded into the background. Rebecca caught her breath, embarrassed by the blush burning her throat and face, and quickly changed the subject. "Do you have any news about Regina? Is she still in a coma?"

"Yes. The doctors don't know what's wrong with her. They can't find anything physical. The old witch is unconscious, and a machine keeps her lungs going. Otherwise, she'd stop breathing," Anastasios said.

"And Alex? How is he?"

"He's withdrawn and refuses to see anyone. Someone from the family takes him food every day as usual."

"So, he's gone back into his shell. You know, him and Hzartanek saved the day," Rebecca said.

"He only seems to come out of his shell when there's a crisis."

"I still see him walking every day."

Anastasios smiled. "That's a given. He walks no matter what's going on around him. So far, he's walked through war, colonialism, and economic crashes. Whatever happens, he keeps on walking."

Rebecca waited until closing time, and Anastasios took her home. Halfway there, he melted into her with a kiss and didn't stop until the following day. Their lovemaking felt entirely natural, as if they'd been together for years and understood each other's bodies intimately without trying. Rebecca felt like she'd found the man she'd been waiting for, and his passionate kisses convinced her he felt the same way. Anastasios left for work in the morning, and Rebecca was so motivated that she finished her paper and finally sent it in for publication. Immediately, a weight lifted off her shoulders.

After all the publicity around Reclamation's coup attempt, Rebecca's classes became unexpectedly popular. She knew how interested students were in parapsychology, but even she was surprised at the attendance rates in her courses and came home tired and happy after three lectures a day.

Anastasios proposed to her on a memorable Thursday night at his bar, and she said yes in front of all his customers. The couple were married six months later in the Archbishopric's church, with Marina as the maid of honour. The happy couple and their guests were surprised when President Omeros turned up in person to congratulate them.

"Our country is grateful to you and Anastasios," he said as he shook their hands at the wedding reception. Rebecca teared up because she still regretted being so headstrong and exposing Reclamation on television. It had almost caused another war, so she'd vowed never to be so arrogant again.

One of the guests approached her during the party and she vaguely remembered him from the university where she worked. Shrewd blue eyes looked into hers, and she noticed he had blond hair and a crooked nose, probably from a childhood accident.

"Congratulations, Rebecca. I hope you'll be happy together. I don't think you remember me; I work at the Dean's office, and my name is Thomas," he said.

"Good to see you, and thanks for coming, Thomas."

"The Dean asked me to speak to you about something important. When will you be back at work?" he said.

"We can talk next Monday; I'll drop by your office," Rebecca said.

"You're not going on a honeymoon?"

"We plan to go after the terms ends."

Thomas looked over his shoulder and leaned in to whisper in her ear. "Please don't forget, it's important." He turned and blended in with the crowd.

The following Monday, burning with curiosity, Rebecca searched for Thomas in the Dean's office. As she approached the office, she heard raised voices and recognised Dean Nicolaou's voice.

"What the hell are we going to do?"

"I have some ideas, just give me some time," Thomas said.

"There IS no time," the dean yelled.

She jumped back as Dean Nikolaou burst out of the room and barrelled down the hallway. "What's wrong with him?" Rebecca said.

"That's what I wanted to talk to you about, the problem that I mentioned at the wedding," Thomas said.

"I've never seen him that angry. Normally, he's so calm."

"He's never been that angry. Come inside. I think you're the only person who can help us with this problem. The university is about to be taken over by the bank, but the circumstances are incredibly unfair," Thomas said.

"What are the circumstances?"

"The bank pumped up our debt with illegal interest rate charges," Thomas said. "We have the forensic proof, but the bank got a court order behind our backs to take over the University's assets. They're sending in an administrator. It'll take years to fight the foreclosure, and the Dean is furious. By this time next month, we could all be out of a job."

Rebecca was nonplussed. "How can the bank take over an asset without good reason?" she said.

"We can prove there's fraud going on, but I don't understand the financials or how they're doing this to us," Thomas said. "Our professor of finance has the proof. All I know is that we're an educational institution and deserve more respect than this."

"I agree it's an enormous injustice. What can I do to help?" Rebecca said.

"We're going to hold a press conference, and we need media contacts and your help. The board of directors remembered how you exposed the coup plot through the media."

Rebecca bit her lip. "Are you sure it's the right thing to do? The last time I did a press conference there was all hell to pay, you must understand that going public can have unexpected consequences," she said.

"We're confident it's the only way left to pursue until the court case goes ahead."

"First, tell me some more details. Who's trying to take over the university?"

Rebecca noticed that Thomas' knuckles were white with tension. "We've learned that the administrator is a financial advisor known for stripping assets and selling them off to his cronies for the lowest price," he said. "The man has mafia connections and runs racehorses besides his financial work, according to our information."

"He's playing a risky game. What's the advisor's name?" Rebecca said.

"Varhaan. He goes everywhere with bodyguards because he probably gets death threats every day."

"What about the banker? Do we have an actual name or just suspicions?"

"Yes, the name we have is Pasianos. We suspect they're working together, and that the whole thing was pre-planned. It happened too quickly for it to be a coincidence," Thomas said.

Rebecca suspected that the bank wanted the university's assets at a bargain price because the buildings were on valuable land next to Nicosia Airport which used to be in the UN buffer zone. The government had abandoned the airport until the Turks withdrew their army and after liberation, the land had quadrupled in value because there were new plans to renovate the airport and re-start operations.

"Somehow, I don't think that a press conference will make much difference. These people have extremely thick skins. They'll just say they have a contract and that they're acting within their rights," Rebecca said.

"What do you suggest?" Thomas said.

"Does the university pay its monthly loan instalments?"

Thomas' eyes narrowed. "Yes, that's why all of this is so surprising. The bank called in its loan without notice and claims that our refusal to pay the whole amount is a breach of contract."

"What does your lawyer say?"

Thomas sighed. "He says that the evidence on our side is strong, and we'll win the court case, but the danger is that while the property is under administration, Varhaan controls everything."

Rebecca crossed her arms. "And he can sell off properties with the bank's agreement while overriding the university's interests," she said.

"Exactly. It's a hostile takeover."

"I'm so sorry to hear about this," Rebecca said. "In this situation we must prove there's a conspiracy to sell assets and get kickbacks from the sales. That's the only possible explanation, and it means that there's a gigantic fraud in action."

Thomas and Rebecca looked at each other in concern. He reached into his desk and handed over a piece of paper. "Here are the full details," he said.

"I have some contacts high in the secret service. I'll ask them for their advice too," she said.

Thomas smiled. "Thanks, you've been a great help and I feel better now. I'll tell the Dean. Maybe he'll calm down."

Rebecca snorted. "He'd better or else his blood pressure will do the bank's work for them. We need him to lead the press conference."

She told Anastasios about the university's debt woes that night over dinner.

"Do you have the names of the bank employees and the lawyer in charge?" he asked.

"Yes, I wrote them down." She handed over a piece of paper with two names on it. "Vaarhan and Pasianos, have you heard of them?" Rebecca said.

Anastasios frowned. "I know of Vaarhan, he's been on the radar for some time on suspicion of financial fraud."

"What kind?"

"The hard-to-prove kind. From what we understand, Vaarhan works with someone in the bank who tips him off with confidential information when an asset-rich company has a loan," he said.

"The bank piles on the interest charges by fiddling the electronic interest rate settings and Vaarhan steps in to foreclose by getting a court order behind the debtor's back. He sells off the assets at bargain prices to his friends who pay him a kickback as a commission."

Rebecca put her fork on the plate as she thought things through. "How can we prove a conspiracy when it all seems in line with the law?" she said.

Anastasios shrugged. "I'm not sure yet. The only way to do it is to get one of his accomplices to inform on him, but that's difficult. He has a highly secretive clique of contacts who know how to keep their mouths shut."

"The university might have to shut down if it doesn't pay off or renegotiate its debt. I could lose my job," she said.

Rebecca stared out of the window onto the wet, narrow road outside their flat on Xanthis Xenierou street in old Nicosia. As had happened so many times, the Light Walker passed by her front window just as she looked outside. Alex's eyes stayed fixed on the ground, and the smoke from his cigarette wafted past his ears and diffused in the streetlight's orange glow. Was it her imagination, or did he tilt his head her way?

The next day, Rebecca told Thomas what she'd learned about Vaarhan and Pasianos. They decided to call the press conference and name names to protect the university.

"They've left us with nothing left to lose," Thomas said.

Two days before the press conference, Vaarhan appeared on the university's grounds flanked by bodyguards and brandishing a court paper. He strode into Thomas' office, pushing Rebecca aside as he approached the desk.

"This property is now under my administration. I expect full cooperation from the senior management and don't even think about questioning my authority. This is a court-ordered administration," Vaarhan said.

Thomas stood up. "We've been expecting you. Wait outside, please. I'm in a meeting," he said.

Vaarhan raised his chin. "No. You wait outside. It is not your office anymore. I'm taking it over for my administration work. This university is about to close its doors, you'd better all start looking for new jobs," Vaarhan said.

Thomas took a deep breath but refused to rise to the bait, motioning Rebecca to follow him. From then on, they worked on the press conference from the Dean's office.

On the day of the press conference, journalists from all the main media channels showed up for the story. Vaarhan tried in vain to prevent it from going ahead, but the dean insisted and he still had the authority. The Dean's speech accused the bank and Vaarhan of conspiracy to defraud the university. The vice-dean had a PhD in finance and backed the Dean's allegations with numbers and facts.

"Our story is the same as many other businesses which face predatory lending and closure because of fraudulent banking practices," the Dean said.

Shortly after the press conference, the Attorney General's office announced a criminal investigation into the bank's actions. Vaarhan didn't show up at the university the next day, but he was waiting at Rebecca's front door that night, flanked by three bodyguards. She halted six meters away from the menacing group.

"What are you doing here?" she demanded as bravely as she could, given her shaking legs.

Vaarhan's small, almost-black eyes narrowed, and his thin lips pursed into wrinkles. He took a step forward on long legs topped by a protruding belly. "I know you're behind the press conference. I came to talk some sense into you and your boss. The university is under administration. You accept that or I'll do something you won't like," he said.

"I can't talk to you. There are legal issues," she said, hearing her voice waver.

One of the bodyguards suddenly moved towards Rebecca and she backed away, tripping and falling over a step. Her back ached where it had hit the ground, and she stared up at the spinning sky, wishing everything would fade away and leave her in peace. A bright light came between Vaarhan and Rebecca, and she glimpsed a shadow within the blaze as the Light Walker stood between her and the goons. She propped herself up on her elbows in time to see Vaarhan and his thugs yelling and trying to block their eyes from the glare of Alex's incredible inner power.

Alex's blurry figure divided into two centers of light against the night's dusky indigo shadows. Rebecca could see another entity, it was Hzartanek extending his energy towards Vaarhan, whose eyes rolled up in their sockets as he fell to the ground. The bully boys ran away, screaming. The ethereal light blinked out, and there was just Alex's slight and hunched figure walking away, a sandwich held loosely in his hand. Rebecca collapsed back onto the ground, where it felt warm and secure.

Strong arms lifted her up, and she opened one tearful eye to see Anastasios.

"Don't worry, love. I'll take care of you. Calm down," he said.

While holding Rebecca, Anastasios called to several nearby secret service agents who picked up the unconscious Vaarhan. As they lifted him into the car, a motorcycle drove by. Popping sounds come from a silenced gun as the driver shot Vaarhan in the chest. The motorcycle zoomed by, and Rebecca felt Anastasios's supportive arms weaken and fall away from her. As she turned, salty blood stung her eyes; the criminals had shot Anastasios! She screamed and then looked around in shock and confusion; was that terrified animal sound coming from her?

The secret service men bundled Anastasios and Rebecca into a sedan and took off at high speed to the hospital. She only felt bruised and shaken up, but Anastasios was struggling for his life. The doctors told her that the bullet had missed his heart by a centimetre and punctured his left lung. The complex operations to save his life took hours, but she stayed until he was out of the operating room and the surgeon told her he was going to be fine.

A secret service agent drove her home at 4:00 am to get some rest after he noticed she was close to collapsing on the hospital floor. On the way home, the agent told her that Vaarhan owed a tremendous amount of money to the gambling mafia. His weakness for horseracing had led to his murder, and he'd almost got Anastasios killed in the crossfire. She fell asleep praying for his recovery.

Rebecca woke up to a leaden stomach and nearly started out of her skin at the sound of the doorbell. What now? The stress of Anastasios' shooting had made a mess of her emotions, but she shook it off as best as she could and opened the door. A stranger was standing outside the house - a nobody, an anybody, who didn't meet her eyes. Dressed in jeans and a blue t-shirt, he could have been any young man walking down the street, except that when his mud-brown eyes finally caught hers, she saw a sly glare in them.

"I have a court paper for you," he said.

"What's this about?"

He sent her another surreptitious sidelong gleam from his mud-brown eyes and handed over some blue papers. "I don't know. My company sent them from the court. Read them and call your lawyer."

She closed the door on his sly face, her chest tightening at the unknown threat. The court papers were in Greek, so it took longer to read them through. After she'd finished reading, her chest felt even tighter, and her hands shook as she made a cup of tea. She'd reached the end of her tether. A lawyer named Profitis was suing her for plotting against the Republic of Cyprus. It was a civil case with a court date set for the day after tomorrow. Profitis was suing Rebecca for what Regina had done to betray the Republic. She felt so angry that she screamed and smashed some plates on the floor. It's not good to repress anger, and breaking plates felt like the safest way to vent her intense outrage at the false accusations.

She called the hospital to ask how Anastasios was feeling, and the nurse gave her the good news that he was awake and wanted to talk to her. When she told him about the legal situation, he started laughing. "Ouch, that hurts," he said.

Relief flooded through her, and she smiled at the thought that he felt better already. "Go ahead, laugh at my problems. It's not funny!" she said.

"It's a non-starter, love," he said. "Don't worry, they're reaching and must be desperate. The entire world knows you are the heroine and Regina is the criminal. We'll go to court with my friend Lefteris. He's an excellent lawyer," Anastasios said.

"But it's a false accusation. How can the lawyer get away with it, and why did the court accept to hear the case?"

"Anyone can sue. All you have to do is file a lawsuit in court. It doesn't mean that it'll stick. For a start, only the Republic has the authority to prosecute someone for treason. The judge will see what a joke this case is because there are many witnesses and so much evidence to the contrary," Anastasios said.

"But there's no time to prepare. The case starts tomorrow. They're tricking me with legal technicalities. If I don't show up, the judge could decide against me," Rebecca said.

"I'll call the lawyer now."

The following day, she went to court with her lawyer, but her accusers didn't appear. It was still a mystery who was accusing her because the summons came from the lawyer's office and had few details. Rebecca's lawyer asked for a 24-hour postponement because of the short notice, and the judge agreed. Somehow, the media found out about the case, and several journalists showed up at the court. One of them asked her whether there was evidence against her. Rebecca's lawyer told her not to answer, even though she was burning inside to reject the claims against her name.

Later, the university Dean called her. "We heard about the court case in the media. What's happening, Rebecca? Are you okay?" he said.

"The allegations are false, Dean. We're going back to court tomorrow to set the record straight," she said.

"Keep me in the loop. Some parents and board members are asking awkward questions, and I'm in a difficult position. The publicity is damaging your reputation and the University's," he said.

"Yes, Dean, I'll contact you when I have more information."

The injustice burned her lungs with pent-up screams of rage. She had worked and suffered to help the Republic thwart another coup and ended up as the target of lies and false accusations. Rebecca realised she could lose her job if the lawyer couldn't restore her reputation.

The next day, the sandstone court buildings were full of journalists, who shoved cameras and microphones in her direction, ignoring the lawyer's 'no comment,' as they walked into the court. This time, the opposing lawyer stood near the entrance. Rebecca's jaw clenched when she saw who his client was. Charlotte Addington was there with blue eyes as cold as ice. The case itself lasted just 15 minutes. Rebecca's lawyer showed several substantial pieces of proof that it was Regina who had plotted against the state, not Rebecca. Because it was a civil suit, the judge ordered Charlotte to pay the costs and dismissed the case.

As they left the courtroom, a woman stepped out from behind a column and Rebecca recognised Regina, who looked half dead. She felt Regina's hatred blazing through her soul. Her baleful eyes burned with malevolence and the waves of black energy were so intense that Rebecca could taste it like poison searing her throat and chest. She turned and shouted at a police officer nearby. "There's an arrest warrant out for this woman!"

As she walked down the court steps towards the officer, Rebecca heard a gunshot and felt something push her arm from behind. The momentum spun her around, and she fell heavily on her side. Another shot rang out and someone started screaming

Rebecca laid on the ground in a daze and couldn't stand up. She felt like a weight was pinning her down on the dusty courtyard as she dragged her arm inch by inch from underneath her body. There was blood on her forearm and shoulder, but she couldn't feel any pain because of the shock.

Later, they told her that Regina had shot her from almost point-blank range. A security officer had knocked Regina's hand away, which was why the bullet went wide and hit her arm instead of her heart. The same security officer had then shot Regina dead.

In the confusion after the attempted coup, Regina had recovered from her coma and sneaked out of the hospital, according to the news programs. She had more than enough money stashed in her hideaway in Dali to help her daughter hire a lawyer to sue Rebecca on false pretences.

The press had recorded Regina's blatant murder attempt on camera, and the international media broadcasted her crime to the world. The court case had been a ploy to get Rebecca out into the open and get a clear shot at killing her mortal enemy, the woman who had thwarted her plans to make another fortune.

The police arrested Charlotte and charged her with being an accomplice to attempted murder. She'd be in prison for several decades on the murder charge alone and would stand trial for treason. The judge refused to accept her lawyer's argument that the treason charge would be double indemnity because of her case against Rebecca. The judge also rejected Charlotte's last-minute insanity plea, so Rebecca hoped she would get life in prison.

Anastasios and Rebecca recovered together in hospital. It would take several weeks of treatment before they could go home, so they whiled away the hours watching news shows of Charlotte coming and going from prison during her trial. It looked like she was going to prison for a long time. Still, something told them that the story wasn't over yet because they'd lost track of the other conspirators. Their foreboding came true. The peace talks between the Greek and Turkish Cypriots were close to completion when Rebecca's journalist friend Ioannis called her in the hospital.

"I heard a rumour about new militant activity in EOKA B and a revival of the TMT and the Grey Wolves. Have you come across any information, Rebecca?" he said.

"No, Ioannis, but I'll make a few calls and get back to you."

"Thanks. Please let me know as soon as you hear something."

She spoke with Anastasios about the conversation with Ioannis, and he promised to investigate it with the Secret Service.

After recovering from their injuries, Rebecca and Anastasios left the hospital together and finally went back home. A few days after their homecoming, Rebecca was at the university when her phone rang. She didn't recognize the number. "Hello, who is this?" she said.

"Hello Rebecca, my name is Marinella. I live with my husband in north Cyprus. I'm concerned about information I heard from my relatives who have connections in the Turkish-Cypriot extremist camp."

"Marinella, I know your name from some stories I heard from the past. You're a peace activist, right?"

"Yes, my husband and I believe in peace for all of Cyprus, for all of humanity. That's what we work for, and our marriage proved that Greek Cypriots could live peacefully with Turkish Cypriots even before liberation."

"I admire your courage and strength. It's difficult to go against social conditioning and follow a vision for peace," Rebecca said.

"It's been tough, but we do it with love and we're satisfied with small steps forward."

"What did you hear about extremism? Was there an incident?"

Marinella paused. "I saw a man in my restaurant in Kyrenia. He was talking to an extremist militant, a member of the Grey Wolves. He seemed familiar, and I showed him to my husband, who remembered him from photographs on television. The man was a suspect in the conspiracy to annex the whole of Cyprus."

"The last I heard, there were a few of them still on the loose," Rebecca said.

"One of them is in north Cyprus as we speak. I'm watching him now," Marinella said.

"They must be up to their old tricks; some things never change. Provocateurs like him caused the tension between the militants in 1974 by turning them against each other with disinformation," Rebecca said.

"We need to be very careful. I can inform my activist network to organize a peace march to send the message that we don't want a repeat of the conflicts," Marinella said.

"Yes, it'd be good timing. I can inform our side to watch the extremists in ELAM and anyone leftover from EOKA B. Can your network organize a simultaneous peace march in the Republic?" Rebecca said.

"I believe so. The bi-communal links are much stronger now, and the peace movement has grown since 2004. I still have faith," Marinella said.

Rebecca promised her new friend that she would be in touch as they said goodbye. Her next call was to Anastasios.

"How are you, love?" he said.

"I'm anxious. I just heard that one of the mercenaries is hiding in the north and talking to the Grey Wolves in Kyrenia."

"Oh Jesus, I'll speak to my boss about it. Do you know where he is now?"

She told him the location of Marinella's restaurant and then drove home to the old city. The autumn light was soft in the late afternoon, gently laying luminous shapes between the shadows of the trees on the road, and she had a curious detached feeling, a premonition that something was waiting around the corner. As she approached her flat, she saw a blond woman standing outside the building. Rebecca heard the sudden sound of soft footsteps to her right, and the Light Walker came from behind, pacing next to her. He strode alongside her until they reached the blond woman, who faced them calmly and held up her hands in placation. Two police officers stood nearby.

"What are you doing here, Charlotte? What do you want?" Rebecca said.

"Please listen to me. I haven't come to harm you or Alexandros. I came to apologise and ask your forgiveness," Charlotte said.

In the twilight, Charlotte appeared fragile and defeated. Her hands shook as she reached them out towards Rebecca. Alex hunched his shoulders and lifted his left hand where there was a ball of light playing in his palm. "I forgive you," Alex said.

Too quickly to see, the light flowed in Charlotte's direction and she closed her eyes with a smile as it entered her body.

"Charlotte, which one of your cronies was talking to Turkish-Cypriot extremists in the north? You must know, so don't lie to me," Rebecca said in a hard voice.

"Rebecca, I apologise to you too. Please forgive me, you must believe I didn't know about my mother's plan to shoot you," Charlotte said. "I know who was talking to the Grey Wolves. You're right that the plan was to disrupt the peace talks. I also heard there was a plan to attack ELAM militants and I've told the police everything I know," Charlotte said.

"What caused the sudden change of heart? Your mother was dead set on controlling Cyprus and ruining what peace there is here," Rebecca retorted. She'd been through too much to accept Charlotte's words at face value.

Charlotte looked down in shame. "I know what my mother did was wrong," she said. "I only want to make amends. I'm cooperating with the authorities to disband her organisation and I've agreed to be a defence witness in any trials that follow. I've already given a written statement about everything my mother planned."

"Regina tried to murder me in broad daylight in front of hundreds of witnesses. It's too difficult to believe you. And where's your father?"

"I don't know," Charlotte said.

Rebecca pushed her hair behind her ear. "Why should I believe that you're any different from your mother?" she said.

"I don't expect you to believe me. But if you can find it in your heart to forgive me, I'd be grateful," Charlotte said. "I know how much damage Regina caused. Everything that's happened has made me ashamed that I'm related to her," Charlotte said with a pleading expression. She pointed to the police officers standing a few meters away. "We're on our way to visit my grandmother so I can make amends with her, too. Would you like to come with us?" Charlotte said.

Rebecca was confused by the sudden turn of events but agreed to the invitation and walked with Charlotte, Alex and the officers to Willow and Leo's house. En route, she called Anastasios.

"You're never going to believe what just happened. Regina's daughter just showed up at our flat and apologized for all the damage her mother caused," she said.

"I know she's turned state's evidence. We've shared the information she gave us about the conspirator in the north. The bi-communal law enforcement unit will handle it," Anastasios said.

The news made Rebecca feel more confident, and she picked up her walking pace. In five minutes, they'd reached Willow's house and Charlotte rang the doorbell. Willow answered the door and took a step back when she saw Charlotte. Her hand went to her mouth, and tears filled her eyes as Leo held her protectively.

"Grandmother, I came to say I'm so sorry for everything. I know my mother scared you and I accept responsibility for my actions. I can't change what happened or the mistakes I made. But I'm different and I'm going to prove it to you. I hope you can find it in your heart to forgive me," Charlotte said.

Alex stepped forward and smiled at Willow. It was a beautiful, rare smile, and her eyes crinkled as she tried to return it.

"I don't know. I need time, Charlotte. Our estrangement went on for too long. Although she was my own daughter, Regina hurt me and everyone I love too much," Willow said.

"I understand. I must go with these police officers, and what I'm going to tell them will send me to prison. Take my word that from now on, you have nothing to fear from me," Charlotte said.

The police officers flanked her, and they walked towards a squad car. Willow watched her go with a wistful expression and wrung her hands. Leo gave her a warm hug. "Don't worry, Willow. Anastasios can arrange for you to visit Charlotte. You can spend some more time with her when you're ready," he said.

Chapter 14

The next day, Marinella's activists marched for peace in the Turkish-Cypriot community and around the whole island. The protests were moving and heartfelt, with people from all of Cyprus' communities walking together. The peace marches had such a strong spirit, and the protesters were so confident about the outcome that their vision of a better future touched all but the hardest of hearts.

On the same day as the marches, the government announced it would hold a peace referendum with the Turkish Cypriots the following week. The agreement called for a federal state with no external guarantors. The Turkish Cypriots would take part in proportion to the size of their community, while keeping a reasonable amount of autonomy when it came to taxes, policing and to governing citizens in a creatively named super district.

The federal government would set up a new property court system to return occupied properties to their original owners. To avoid homelessness and poverty, the authorities would find homes for the families who would have to leave their houses. Without Turkey's interference and funding for extremist groups, a common-sense agreement with respect for human rights on both sides appeared to be within reach. Meanwhile, Cyprus launched a long overdue lawsuit in the

Hague against Turkey for human rights violations and war crimes in 1974.

The police rounded up several militants based on the information Charlotte confessed to them, hoping to avoid any clashes between nationalist groups. But there was still considerable resistance to peace between the Greek-and-Turkish Cypriots, and the media in both communities reported wide political differences in public opinion.

On the day of the referendum, the polls predicted that the public wouldn't approve of the peace plan because the division between the two communities had been a reality for too long. Decades of division and non-communication had entrenched attitudes, and a quick change was unlikely. The recent conflict with Turkey had scared many people into taking the 'no' side. When Rebecca voted 'yes' in a nearby school, she saw the Light Walker gliding past the polling station, seeming to glow with an internal power. Later, people told her he had walked across many Nicosia districts, always past polling stations. Was he walking with Hzartanek?

After an anxious night, the poll results came in the early morning hours of the next day. A slight majority of Cypriots had voted 'yes' to the reunification plan, putting their trust in a better future than the past. The result was a complete surprise to journalists and politicians given that the polls had been so negative. By now, even Anastasios believed that Alex had higher powers and had worked to spread light, peace and trust when he walked around the polling stations in Nicosia.

It took another three years for the reunification plan to be passed through the legislature, and the Greek-and-Turkish

225

Cypriots came to live in a United Federal Cyprus, or simply Cyprus, but a long, arduous journey lay ahead for the island. The federal government's Truth and Reconciliation Commission worked hard to settle individual cases and it raised awareness of the importance of community peace and unity for all Cypriots. But political life was as contentious as ever, with lingering power struggles and complex feelings from past wars. The peace was so fragile it could have been broken at any moment.

Everyday life was easier for travelling to the Turkish-Cypriot super district and as time went on, the differences between the communities faded and become more intangible. Turkish-and-Greek Cypriot businesses used the court system to settle any claims, and the country appeared to be on its way to a mature democracy, overcoming its tragic conflicts. They solved legal and political differences in a way that Rebecca could only describe as miraculous.

Over time, family ties grew between the Greek-and-Turkish Cypriots, giving birth to a new generation who lived in a united country. Young Cypriots related only distantly to their country's past conflicts, much like the Europeans related to the Napoleonic Wars. Over time, the disputes faded into the past. As younger generations grew up in a peaceful environment, they marginalised and ignored the extremist elements which had caused so much damage. New laws protected ethnic differences and cultural history. Legal scholars considered the rules to be some of the most enlightened and effective in the world, and the Greek-and-Turkish Cypriot leaders who had jointly brokered the reunification deal won the Nobel Peace Prize.

Problems persisted, though. There was always an uncomfortable sense that Turkey was watching over Cyprus' shoulder for any missteps, and its ally, the UK, still had an airbase near Limassol. Still, the Cypriots had reunited by choice and were finally in charge of their destiny.

Work and life with Anastasios kept Rebecca busy. Her marriage to Anastasios was everything she'd ever dreamed of in a relationship. She still hadn't fallen pregnant after three years, but not even that could cloud their happiness. Her gynaecologist had told her they were both fit and healthy and she should be more patient. Anastasios brushed off her concerns with a hug and a long kiss. "Even if we never have children, I'm just happy we're together, Rebecca. I love you. Please stop worrying. Stress will only delay things. It's in God's hands if we have children," he'd say.

Subconsciously Rebecca kept a lookout for the Light Walker, but he didn't show up as often as he used to, so maybe he'd changed his route or his routine. One day, their paths crossed outside Rebecca's flat, and she approached him slowly, keeping her distance so as not to frighten him.

"Alexandros, can we please talk?" she said.

Alex dropped his gaze to the tarmac and hunched his shoulders slightly, then nodded.

"Thank you for trusting me. Is it okay to ask you some questions? Is Hzartanek still with you?" Rebecca said.

Alex nodded.

"Can you describe him to me?"

"He's one and all. He's pure light," Alex said.

"How did it feel when you became consumed by his light, when you projected it all around you?"

"It was warm and pulled out of me like the tide."

"Did it hurt?"

"No. The light shone through me, and I felt my cells disappear into it."

"And what about your maths? Do you still practice?"

Alex shook his head. "There's no need for maths since I'm part of the calculation and I control the calculation," he said.

"I see. So, you feel you understand the mathematical laws of nature?" Rebecca said.

"I'm part of them and so are you."

"There's a plan, a formula? How do you control the calculation?"

"By balancing one side with the other."

"And how does that work, Alexandros?"

But by then, Alex had put his cigarette back into his mouth and walked away with his head bowed, a sandwich in a plastic bag held loosely by his side. Rebecca shook her head and smiled, realising this was the first time she'd had a conversation with Alex. After everything they'd been through together, she was eager to talk with him again. She had so many questions and speaking with Alex could be her only chance to gather more empirical evidence of a greater power and its intentions. She desperately wanted to see the universe's real magic and understand the mysteries and miracles that were so astonishing to human beings but were just the everyday workings of a mighty and infinite cosmos.

Although she looked out for the Light Walker passing by on their street, it was another month before she saw Alex again during a visit to Leo and Willow Carter's home. She spotted him in the expansive garden, sitting far away from the group near a pruned hedge. Rebecca walked over and stood at least two meters away to avoid triggering his fear of close contact. "Hello, Alex, how are you?" she said.

Alex avoided her eyes and looked down at the lawn and she sensed his misery.

"Is Hzartanek with you?"

"No."

"Why not? What happened? Where did he go?"

"He's gone, he told me the sphere is in balance and it doesn't need him here anymore. It doesn't need me either. That's what he said before he left me."

Alex's head drooped, and he looked so sad she had to stop herself from giving him a reassuring hug. Touching Alex would not be a good idea, it would frighten him.

"I'm sorry to hear that. Are you lonely without Hzartanek?" Rebecca said.

"Yes, I miss his mind whispers, and I don't know where to walk now."

"Did he say goodbye?"

"No, I woke up, and he was gone. No whispers, no walking quests, nothing left. Leave me alone," he said.

Rebecca walked back to the table, wondering what she could do to help Alex, who had helped so many people and expected nothing in return. Over the following weeks, she watched out for him, hoping to talk to him, but he'd stopped walking on her road, and she didn't see him on his daily walks anywhere in the neighbourhood. One evening, she heard a knock on her front door. When she opened it, Alex stood on her doorstep, a beatific smile on his face.

"Rebecca, I came to say goodbye. Hzartanek is back. He told me where to walk. I'll travel with him to another sphere in the 17th dimension."

"I'm so happy for you."

Alexandros made an odd sign with his hands, clasping them together and rocking them at the level of her belly.

"Please tell your baby about me and love him as you love me. Goodbye, Rebecca. Remember I will always find you through our cosmic connection," he said.

"My baby? What do you mean, Alex? I haven't been able to get pregnant."

But Alex didn't answer, and it was the last thing he ever said to her in person. He turned and walked up the curving road that led to the OXI roundabout, growing smaller and more distant with each step. Alexandros' figure gradually merged with the shadows and light at the top of the road, and as she watched, the Light Walker glided off the surface of the road and floated over the fountain dancing on the roundabout. The last she saw of him was insubstantial light, like a firefly hovering over the city. Next to him, she could just make out Hzartanek's rainbow light merging with his.

Suddenly, a strange, serpentine darkness twisted around their faint shapes and eclipsed their shining sparks of light. Her tears blurred out the impression of Alex and Hzartanek leaving the world forever to go to another, and perhaps a better, place. She knew she'd miss his daily walks and protection, but her heart and spirit felt that he was still deeply connected to her in the quantum ocean, where communication has no limits and where love spans the infinite universe.

Not long after, Rebecca had a dream that Alex was sitting with her parents on a bright green field. They were holding each other and smiling. Alex turned to her and made a cradle from his hands again. Something told her to do a pregnancy test for no other reason than the dream. When the double pink line appeared, she could hardly believe it was positive. Alex's prediction had turned out to be true. She gave birth nine months later, and they named their baby Alexandros after their unsung hero, the Light Walker.

Alexandros was barely two years old when he started counting. Their son astonished them with his first feat of counting from zero to one thousand by writing the numbers even before he could talk. Soon after that, he said '17, one, three, 17,' and gave his parents a toothless grin. Anastasios and Rebecca smiled at each other. They already knew what he meant. She took seventeen steps to the kitchen sink, picked one glass from the cabinet, ran the water for three seconds and walked seventeen steps back to her son's chair with a glass of water.

The cosmos had blessed them with a child prodigy named Alexandros, their very own Light Walker. They watched and marvelled at his abilities, which started with mathematics and blossomed into physics and biology. Baby Alexandros was a bright and happy child, engaged with everything around him. As she watched him play with his toys, Rebecca felt it was as if the universal synchronicity she saw at every turn had given the Light Walker a second chance at a happy life.

Chapter 15

Rebecca woke up strapped to a bed in a white room with nothing else in sight except a locked door with bolted padlocks and fire drill instructions on the wall. The straps were firm but not tight, and she knew she couldn't struggle against them. She felt an eerie calm as if she'd just left a long, dark corridor full of monsters and a sunlit room was at the end. The last thing she could remember was watching over baby Alexandros as he played with his toy horse. The door opened, and a woman dressed in a white doctor's uniform walked in with a smile on her familiar face.

"Marina, what are you doing here? Where am I?" Rebecca said. Her throat hurt when she talked, and it was painful to swallow.

"My dear, my name's not Marina. I'm Dr Stephanou, don't you remember me? You're my patient. We're in Athalassa Psychiatric Clinic," she said.

"You're not Marina? What are you saying? Have you lost your mind? Why am I strapped to the bed?"

"Rebecca, it's for your own safety. You had a psychotic break and were completely out of control. How do you feel now?"

"I feel calm. How long have I been in this place, and why do you keep telling you're not my oldest friend? We had lunch the day before yesterday, for God's sake. Why are you lying to me?"

The doctor paused and scrutinized Rebecca. "I'm afraid you've confused me with someone else. You've been here for many years, my dear, since 1998," she said. "I consider you a friend, but we didn't know each other before you came here. This place is your home, and when you're calm, you have friends here, you're happy."

Rebecca clutched at the sheet. "This is insane. What about my husband, Anastasios, and my child, Alexandros?" she said, stuttering over the words.

"You never married or had children, dear Rebecca. You're a paranoid schizophrenic patient here. Sometimes you forget things after a psychotic break. You should remember this from your psychology degrees."

"So, I'm a psychologist. That part is true?" Rebecca said.

"Yes, you were a brilliant psychologist, and when you're feeling well, we talk a lot about our work."

"Why doesn't the medication work on me? You're saying someone put me into a mental institution for over a decade?"

Dr. Stephanou made a soothing gesture. "Stay calm. Yes, we keep trying new drugs. They work for a while, and then they stop working, and you lose track of reality. Your delusions are incredibly complex."

"Am I dangerous, Marina, I mean, Dr Stephanou?"

"Not to anyone but yourself. We've seen you go through terrible seizures and hallucinations, but you only harm yourself, never anyone else."

"What about the Cyprus problem? Is it solved?"

"No, my dear, it's intractable and always was. Nothing's changed. Since you're awake and calm, you need to understand that it's one of your fixations."

"And the Light Walker? Is he another figment of my imagination? What about the third invasion of Cyprus?" Rebecca's voice rose.

"I haven't heard you talk about them before. These are new delusions," the doctor said.

"You must think I'm stupid. I don't believe a word you're saying. What's going on? What could you possibly gain by gaslighting me in this way?" Rebecca jerked against the straps.

"Don't get upset again. If you stay calm, I'll unstrap you."

Rebecca stopped squirming. "Yes, sorry, please unstrap me. I feel suffocated, I'm panicking."

After the doctor had finished unstrapping her, Rebecca sat up on the bed. She closed her eyes, and when she opened them, the doctor was no longer there. The eerie calmness returned now that she was alone. She looked over her shoulder. She smelled a rat. Someone was playing tricks on her, and she was determined to find out who it was. She summoned the Light Walker with her mind. Even though he was light-years away in the 17th dimension, their entangled consciousnesses quickly communicated across the distance.

"We have to find Hzartanek. Reclamation has come back and kidnapped me," she mind spoke.

"Rebecca, are you sure? You're telling me that the sphere is unbalanced again? We didn't sense anything," Alex mind spoke.

"The sphere is unbalanced. We must save Cyprus again. The tyrants are up to their old tricks. I'm trapped in a mental institution, but I don't believe what the doctor tells me."

"How do you know what the doctor said is not true? Perhaps you do have a mental illness," Alex mind spoke.

His question made her pause and question how exactly could she prove her reality? The symptoms of schizophrenia closely mirror real experiences and feelings. That's why people with schizophrenia have difficulty knowing what's real and what's not. She looked at her right arm, remembering a slight bend in the bone where she'd broken it after the would-be assassin rammed into the Secret Service car. The curve in the bone wasn't there. This was impossible! She knew who she was, and nothing would convince her otherwise.

Rebecca heard a second voice: "You'll never prove what's real." The voice sounded familiar. She looked around the sterile, white room and saw that the wall was jittering and undulating. A blond woman emerged from the wall, smiling brightly at her.

"Remember me?"

Rebecca's scream split the air between them, and the shockwave travelled so hard and fast that the woman wavered, then disintegrated. She sobbed into her hands, hunching her shoulders and curling up on the hard bed. When she'd calmed down, Rebecca communed with Hzartanek and Alex again. "Alex, I need to exchange consciousness with you for a while. It might help me understand what's going on," she mind spoke.

"Yes, you're allowed to for a limited time, not over three milliseconds," Hzartanek mind spoke. The consciousness switch was instantaneous, and she found herself in Alex's consciousness on the other side of the universe. The 17th dimension was full of spheres and orbs. Everything was round and her consciousness bobbed in and out of the spheres as she communed with Hzartanek.

"What happened to my life?" she mind spoke.

"You are in an alternate reality. Somehow, your consciousness has shifted."

"How am I going to get back? Anastasios needs me, so does my baby."

"As far as they're concerned, you're still in the original reality. You haven't disappeared from your family's lives."

"But what about my consciousness?"

"It's altered. We cannot tell you what happened."

"How do I get back to my life? How do I find out what happened?"

"You would have to heal your chronic paranoia and schizophrenia in the alternate reality. Your consciousness might merge back with your own life, or at least, the life you most want if you heal," Hzartanek mind spoke.

"I don't think I can do it."

A bracelet of pure platinum appeared on her wrist, shining subtly.

"Take this and use it to harness your fears whenever they become too much," Hzartanek mind spoke.

The three milliseconds had run out, and she was back in her room in the mental institution. Rebecca clenched her fist and pounded it on her leg. It hurt, snapping her back into reality, and her head felt clearer.

I have to get a hold of myself and try to heal my mind; she muttered.

When Dr. Stephanou came back with some anti-psychotic pills, she asked her to stay and talk with her for a while. "Doctor, I want to heal my mind so I can leave the institution. From what I remember, schizophrenia is chronic but treatable if I cooperate."

"Yes, Rebecca, we still believe we can treat you. Your case is unique because you don't respond to medication for more than five or six days. That makes your mental health situation more precarious," the doctor said.

"So, sometimes my mental health is good?" Rebecca said.

"Yes, it's extraordinary. You seem like a different person, more like your normal character. During those times, you study your psychology books and seem to enjoy life. You even help us with other patients, as a fully qualified psychologist your suggestions are right on the money."

"And then what happens?"

"You change, you hallucinate events and people that don't exist, often with tiny details, almost like a parallel life. The stories you tell me are uncanny, much more precise than other schizophrenics I've treated," the doctor said.

"Do I have anyone special in my life, family, friends?"

"My dear Rebecca, you have your parents, don't you remember? They come to visit you every fortnight when you're well and you're willing to communicate with them."

"My parents are alive?" Rebecca couldn't stop smiling. It was like a dream come true, finally, a welcome miracle.

"They're alive, sometimes I have to keep reminding you," Dr. Stephanou said. "It's part of your delusion that they died in a plane accident. When you're not feeling well, you refuse to see your parents because you think we're playing a trick on you."

"When will they come again?" Rebecca said.

"They're due for a visit the day after tomorrow. You can talk to them then," the psychiatrist said as she gave her a laptop to write her thoughts in a journal as part of her therapy. Once the medication kicked in, Rebecca's mind became even more precise, and she wrote herself a reminder of something important.

'Reality two is not your reality. Heal your mind to return to your original reality.'

Two days later, she greeted her parents with tears and enormous hugs, grasping them both to her as if they'd returned from the dead, which to her, they had. Her father gently disentangled himself, his blue eyes tender and filled with tears. "Rebecca, my love, it's so good to see you're feeling well today," her father said.

Her mother gave her another impulsive hug, and Rebecca breathed in the soft vanilla scent of her skin and hair. She was wearing a green dress and open-toed sandals. Her head only came up to Rebecca's shoulders. She'd grown so fast when she was little that she was taller than her mother by the time she was 12 years old. They sat outside in the tree-lined hospital yard and drank tea. Rebecca asked them if they had any family news. They told her that her aunt had remarried for the third time, and they all laughed fondly; her aunt was notoriously flighty, and each of her marriages ended in a flurry of extramarital affairs and hurt feelings. Somehow, her aunt always stayed friends with her exes.

Rebecca's mother gave her five books on psychology to read, and she smiled at the gift. "Thanks, Mum, they'll keep me busy. I'll heal myself, no matter what it takes," Rebecca said.

"That's the spirit, darling. You can do it."

Rebecca's father threw his wife a warning look. "The doctors will tell us what to do, Myriam. Rebecca has to follow their instructions to get better," he said.

A slim man walked past their table, dressed in a beautiful suit made of a dark, plush material. Rebecca couldn't repress a gasp and she pushed her chair back to run to him. "Alex, is it you?" she said.

The man who turned to look at her was Alex, but - he wasn't Alex. In reality two, he was distinguished and carried himself with a successful and confident attitude. The faraway look in his eyes was familiar to her, though. He didn't have time to answer her question because Rebecca's parents rushed to pull her away from him and three orderlies ran towards them before her father calmed them down. "It's okay, she just thought he was a friend of ours," he told the orderlies as they took Rebecca back to their table.

"Rebecca, you can't just run up to people like that. Do you know who he is?" her mother said.

"No, who is he? Is it Alexandros Kyprianides?"

"Yes. He's a famous mathematician and scientist, as famous as Einstein in scientific circles," her father said.

"So, he's a famous scientist in this reality," Rebecca said with a pensive expression.

Her parents exchanged an anxious look. "What do you mean, Rebecca? I hope you are not starting again with the delusions and imaginings. We know they're part of your illness," her father said.

"But Rebecca, how did you know his name?" her mother asked.

"I can't explain everything right now. Let's just spend our time together talking about pleasant things. Tell me more about Auntie Elena's latest husband. Is he rich?" Rebecca said with a smile.

Her parents agreed with relief, and the rest of the visit went well. After they left, she got the chance to ask an orderly what Alex was doing there. "He visits his mother; she's been here for decades suffering from clinical depression," the orderly answered.

Rebecca used the hospital's virtual reality room to research Alex's stratospheric career. He was celebrated everywhere for being a mathematical genius and he had three PhDs. One of his breakthroughs was in 1992 when he invented a machine which measured quantum activity in the brain and recorded communication between entangled particles. He called it the Soul Tracker.

Rebecca remembered her mission to prove parapsychology and her hopes rose that, in this reality, there was technology that could help her. The first task was to find out who Alex's mother was and locate her room in the clinic. It didn't take her long to persuade the orderly who liked her to share the information that Alex's mother was on the floor beneath hers in room 211.

The minute she had a chance, she ran down to room 211 to speak to Alex's mother. But the woman she encountered couldn't talk to anyone. She was painfully thin and almost catatonic in her bed, only moving to groan about her aching back. When Rebecca asked about her son, she stared at her blankly. Rebecca would have to find another way to reach reality-two Alex. In the end, he reached her. There was a knock on her door on day, and Rebecca's doctor and Alex walked in together and stopped at the foot of her bed.

"Rebecca, this is Dr Alexandros Kyprianides. He asked to meet you to discuss why you think you know him," Dr. Stephanou said.

Alexandros looked at her with narrowed brown eyes through thick glasses. For the moment, he had focused entirely on Rebecca with eyes full of intelligence and she saw a communicative humour that reality one Alexandros didn't have. He took her hand gently in his warm hands. "Rebecca, it's nice to meet you," he said.

"Alex, it's good to meet you in this reality. I already know you from a different one," Rebecca said.

Alexandros looked interested. "What's the other reality like?" he said.

Dr Stephanou frowned and shot him a look. "I doubt we should entertain Rebecca's delusions. It could trigger an episode," she said.

"I'm curious about her experiences, even if they're imaginary," Alexandros said. "Rebecca knew my name and seemed to know me as a person when she ran up to me the other day. What's even odder is that I feel like I know her. I'd like to understand more."

Rebecca told them the story of Alexandros' alter ego in her reality and that he was a brilliant mathematician who went through the hell of bullying and attempted murder when he was young. "You rose above it all, Alexandros. You rose above it all," she said after telling them the whole story.

Alexandros and the psychiatrist went quiet when she finished. "The amount of detail is just incredible, and your story feels so familiar to me," Alexandros said.

"It's always been that way with Rebecca's delusions. She is utterly convincing until she hurts herself during one of her episodes," Dr Stephanou said.

"And how do you feel now?" Alexandros asked.

"I feel clear today. I'm anxious about my family back in my reality. Could you help me with one of the devices you invented? Perhaps you could transport my consciousness back to my real body," Rebecca said.

Alexandros assured her that he would think about the possibility and left with the psychiatrist. The following days passed slowly. She occupied herself with writing in her journal and felt grateful for her parents, who sent her a gift basket with her favourite chocolates and candy. She was excited when Alexandros finally asked to see her again and agreed immediately. He arrived wearing his usual dark suit and crisp white shirt.

"Alexandros, you certainly dress better than your alter ego, Alex. He walked around in tramp clothes," she said.

He smiled and took out a slim, white metal object. "I don't know how familiar you are with quantum physics, but briefly, there have been massive advances in the science of consciousness," Alexandros said.

"Where I'm from, there are advances in the study of quantum particles, but not in the study of consciousness as a hard science," Rebecca said.

"Interesting. I thought about what you said, and I'd like to run a test on the quantum activity in your brain if that's okay with you," Alexandros said.

"Yes, I'll try anything. What will the test results mean?"

"The device is called Soul Tracker, and it can record the quantum activity in your brain and the entangled particles elsewhere in the cosmos," Alexandros said.

"That's amazing."

Alexandros passed the device over her head and checked the display. "Interesting. Your Q - or quantum activity - is unusual. It appears to be isolated to your brain. Normally, Q connects to particles in other parts of the universe, the Source of the original spark. That's how consciousness travels," he said.

"So, something has blocked my Q."

"Exactly. Well done, Rebecca, that's it in a nutshell."

Rebecca looked confused. "And how does that affect me?" she said.

"The universe is in constant communication with itself, Rebecca. If your soul isn't communicating with the Source, it means something has gone wrong. The question is, how do we fix a split consciousness?"

"A split consciousness? I've heard of a split personality but not of a split consciousness," Rebecca said.

"I just made it up," Alexandros said with a grin.

"It fits," she replied with an answering smile.

"Communication between particles in the quantum field is a natural phenomenon," he said. "If your consciousness splits, we must reconnect it with its twinned particles. That's how reality becomes tangible, by connecting and building particle fields. If we don't heal your consciousness, no medication can help you."

"Okay, how do we do that, and what might happen?"

"Soul Tracker can only measure Q. It can't do anything else. I need to think about a solution, but it'll take some time," Alexandros said.

"I can wait. I have nothing else but time on my hands," she said.

"What we need is a device that can identify the twinned particles of your consciousness and reconnect them with your current reality," Alexandros said. "It's never been done before, and I don't know what might happen. One of my colleagues is working on an invention that might help. Are you willing to sign a disclaimer?"

Rebecca shrugged. "Yes. I have nothing to lose, except for life in a mental health institution," she said.

Alexandros left, promising to come back when he had news. Two weeks later, he came into her room accompanied by another man holding a device. The device was much bigger than the Q instrument. It looked like a box with a shallow dip in the centre of the lid. Alexandros introduced his colleague as Dr Tamoresky, a quantum mechanics physicist from Russia. Tamoresky was taller than Alexandros and haphazardly dressed in an off-center yellow tie and grey suit. The pale blue eyes peering short-sightedly through round glasses seemed friendly enough.

"Dr Tamoresky's device is an ultra-sophisticated particle collider. He wants to change it so that instead of causing particles to collide, it makes them entangle. If it works, your consciousness will be whole again and you might return to your primary reality," Alexandros said.

"I believe it can work. Are you willing to give it a chance?" Dr Tamoresky said in a thick Russian accent.

"What could go wrong?" she said with a smile.

"That's my girl, bravo Rebecca, we're making history here," Alexandros said.

Tamoresky displayed a complete lack of humour. "No jokes, please, this is serious experiment. Today, I want to measure your head. Please lay it on my device, there, in the hollow," Tamoresky said. He took the measurements, and the scientists left with promises that they would return as soon as possible.

While she waited, Hzartanek and the Light Walker communed with Rebecca from the 17th dimension. "I need to warn you about Cataclysm," Hzartanek mind spoke.

"Who is Cataclysm?" Rebecca mind spoke.

"What, not who. Cataclysm is a force of dark energy. My species is a harmonizer and balancer in the Universe. Cataclysm is the divider, the destroyer. Wherever we are, so are they. It is the way of the cosmos."

"Why are you warning me now?"

"Cataclysm might have caused the split in your consciousness."

"You mean I have dark energy living inside me?"

"Dark energy is all around us, but it seems to affect some people more than others," Hzartanek mind spoke.

"Thank you for the warning. What should I do if I come across Cataclysm? How will I know what it is?" Rebecca mind spoke.

"Use your bracelet. It will gather in all fears and dissipate them. Dark energy grows with the energy of fear, so the bracelet will help you to be courageous."

Rebecca looked down at her wrist where the bracelet shone against her skin. The communions with Hzartanek and the Light Walker comforted her, but she was afraid that the split in her consciousness was getting worse and might become permanent.

Tamoresky and Alexandros' next visit came many weeks later, and the wait made her more anxious than ever. They walked in with the same box-like devices and set up the experiment to merge her consciousness across time and space. She was nervous and fidgeted too much, and they told her to calm down, but the scientists' reassurances didn't work, in fact, they made her even more anxious. Then Rebecca touched her bracelet and felt the fears drain away. Her whole body relaxed, and the scientists nodded their approval.

"Please lay your head on top of the device," Tamoresky said.

After she laid her head down, Tamoresky positioned the second device parallel to the first one and used a remote control to switch them on. She felt a slight vibration beneath her head, but nothing else. Suddenly, the room seemed to undulate, and a crack appeared in the air just below the ceiling. Darkness poured in and covered the white walls, turning them dirty grey. When she looked at the scientists, their expressions were unchanged and they hadn't noticed anything different in the room.

"Please try to keep your head straight," Tamoresky said.

She touched her bracelet again and the Cataclysm receded through the crack in the ceiling as her courage drowned her fears. The bracelet helped to banish her terror. Small victories were better than none and the room went back to a regular, solid-state version of reality.

"Rebecca."

Anastasios' voice came from far away, and she felt spaced out, disconnected. Time had slowed down.

"Rebecca, can you hear me?"

Anastasios' concerned face appeared above hers. She was no longer in the reality-two psychiatric clinic but in her home in old Nicosia. A split second later, she was back in the reality two clinic, and the scientists were staring at her like she was a laboratory rat. It had worked! She was back home in her consciousness for a split second before the dark force snatched her away from her family again.

The disappointment felt like a punch in the stomach: "Stop looking at me like that," she said.

"Sorry, Rebecca, we were just worried about you," Alexandros said.

"We spent the last two minutes trying to revive you. You had no pulse, no heartbeat," Tamoresky said.

"It worked. I was back in my original consciousness. I saw my husband, Anastasios. He's worried about me."

Alexandros took her hand lightly. "If the procedure works, then it means you must die in this reality to heal your split consciousness. Are you ready to do that?" Alexandros said.

She took a deep breath and returned the pressure on his hands. "Yes, I'm ready. I don't want to live like this. If I have to die to get back to my husband and child, I'll take the risk."

Tamoresky paced the room. "What if it doesn't work, and Rebecca dies in this reality, only to die in her original reality as well?" he said. "This is too risky, Alexandros. You know how much I respect you, but I cannot proceed. Everyone will blame her death on my machine. I'll lose my reputation." The scientist was adamant and refused to budge, despite Rebecca's pleas and assurances.

"There's another question we must ask, Rebecca," Alexandros said. "What if your consciousness leaves this body and doesn't make it to the body in your original time and space? We stopped just in time to prevent you from dying. On the next attempt, there'll be no going back," Alexandros said.

Rebecca started crying. The crying became hysteria, and she banged her arms on the table hard enough to bruise the skin. The men immediately exchanged uncomfortable looks.

"We'll find another way, Rebecca. Give me some time to think," Alexandros said on his way out as a nurse rushed in with some medication.

"Calm down, calm down, this will help," the nurse said.

The tranquilliser knocked her out for several hours, and she felt woozy for another three days, but biting anxiety grew beneath the clouds in her mind. Would she ever go back to her home? She couldn't bear the weight of two lives at the same time.

Alexandros took a long time to return to the clinic and his face lit up when he saw her sitting at the table reading a book. "Rebecca, I'm glad to see you feel better. I published a paper with my theory about split consciousness, and a professor of microbiology contacted me with some promising news that could help your case," he said.

"What's the news, Alexandros? Will it help me get back to reality one?"

"Yes, I believe it will. Professor Steinfeld developed a machine that can heal damaged brain networks. He proposes to use it to scan and heal your mind. This could restore your consciousness to its normal duality and communication with the quantum ocean," Alexandros said.

"Why did it take you so long to come back? You know how slowly time goes when you're locked up in a hospital."

"I'm sorry, Rebecca, my wife had a health problem, and we had to run some tests."

"You're married?"

"Yes, we have three children. My wife's name is Elena."

"Sorry if I seem surprised. The Alex I knew in reality one never even had a girlfriend, as far as I know," she said.

"I can understand your surprise. The quantum world works in weird ways, but you are the first person I've met who's split from their reality and remembers it."

"Why do you believe me? The doctors say I am a schizophrenic. All of this could be in my mind."

"Your thoughts are clear and organised. What you've described is too detailed to be a hallucination. I have a strong feeling that I know you and that we shared experiences together."

Alexandros sat opposite her at the table and leaned forward. "I need you to think back in time, Rebecca. We must pinpoint the exact memory when you split from your original consciousness," he said.

Rebecca clicked her fingers on the bedside table. "My last memory is of bringing my son a glass of water. We called him Alexandros after you. He's also a mathematical genius."

"But he's not me."

"No, he just has some of your abilities. His personality and character are completely different. The man I knew as Alex the Light Walker disappeared one day with his protector, Hzartanek."

Alexandros looked at her with keen interest. "Where did they go?"

"To the 17th dimension. Hzartanek is a cosmic force, a balancer and harmony bringer. They turned into light and changed dimensions."

Alexandros became more intent: "Think back. This was a cosmic event, a merging of dimensions. Did something else happen at the same time?"

It took her a moment to remember. "There was a weird darkness around their spirits as they left our dimension."

"A darkness?"

Rebecca sat up, her eyes wide. "Yes, this must be Cataclysm. It's the opposing force to Hzartanek's ability to balance the Universe," she said.

"Do you communicate with Cataclysm in the same way as you do with Hzartanek?"

"No, I haven't had contact with this force, although I saw something in my room when we tried to merge my consciousness."

"What did you see?"

"A crack in the ceiling and dark energy that looked like mist. Hzartanek gave me this bracelet to give me the courage to get rid of my fears. Cataclysm energies feed on fear," Rebecca said.

"I need to think about what this means," he said. Alexandros sat back, and she read her book as he contemplated their next move. She clicked her fingers on the table again, and Alexandros covered her hand with his.

"Rebecca, your fidgeting is distracting. Please, could you stop until I think things through?"

"Sorry."

"If the microbiologist's treatment works to fix the problem in your brain, you could revert to your natural state and return to your true reality," he mused.

"But what about Cataclysm?"

"Yes, that's another problem. If the dark energy has a chance, it'll interfere with the transition, and your consciousness will remain split."

"I'm willing to try it. Like I said before, I have nothing to lose, not even my sanity, apparently."

Alexandros patted her hand and crossed his arms as he leaned back in his chair. "I want to place a Q tracker in your brain. It won't hurt you or change anything. All it will allow me to do is to communicate with you across alternate realities if our experiment works," Alexandros said.

"That's ok with me. How will I know we're communicating?"

"You'll feel my presence, and I'll communicate in images and with my thoughts," Alexandros said.

"That's how I commune with Hzartanek. Do I have to do anything?"

"No, I'll read your thoughts and record them on my device," Alexandros said.

"Will you be spying on me the whole time? I'm not sure I like that. Will my privacy disappear?"

"No, I'll only activate the connection with your permission. I can only communicate with one neural network in your brain, and I'll program it to be isolated unless we're mind speaking," Alexandros said. "If the experiment works to restore your consciousness to the correct realities, the first time I contact you will be on your New Year's Day. I have no other interest except making sure you're okay."

"I see. Well, it might not work anyway," Rebecca said.

They set the date for the experiment with the microbiologist for Saturday, and Rebecca spent the days feeling agitated and asking to see her parents. If they reconnected her consciousness, she would never see them again. But her parents sent her a message that they were travelling to France.

On Saturday, Alexandros walked into her room with a short, bespectacled man wearing a red shirt and jeans. "Rebecca, meet one of my colleagues, Dr Steinfeld," Alexandros said.

Steinfeld's blue eyes twinkled at her as he shook her hand. "Good to meet you, Rebecca. You're a brave one to agree to our little experiment," Steinfeld said.

She caught a slight accent and asked him how and why he was in Cyprus. "In our reality, it's a world centre for microbiology and other sciences. It's like Switzerland for banking," he answered.

"Well, at least one thing's the same. Switzerland is also a banking centre where I'm from, but Cyprus was only getting started as a centre for the sciences when my consciousness split," she said.

"I wish we had more time to talk. It's fascinating that your consciousness exists in two different realities. We knew about the possibility of a multiverse but never had solid proof," Steinfeld said.

The scientists placed three rubber pads on her head. The pads connected wirelessly to a long, narrow black instrument. "I'll talk you through this, Rebecca. My instrument scans your brain for broken networks. Then it recreates any missing parts of the neural net," Steinfeld said.

"We usually use it to heal people with Alzheimer's disease or patients with amnesia," Alexandros said.

"What an incredible instrument. We could use it in reality one. Alzheimer's is a leading cause of dementia and death," Rebecca said.

"It occurred to me that if the experiment works, we should communicate so that scientists in your reality can benefit from our technology," Alexandros said.

"In both realities, you're a truly kind person, Alexandros. I can help set that up with my university," she said.

"Thank you. If this works, it means goodbye. I'll reach out to you by consciousness travel. Remember, New Year's Day," Alexandros said, motioning her to lie down.

"Try to relax, Rebecca. It's time to heal the neural networks in your brain," Steinfeld said.

She touched her bracelet and felt calmer than she had in days. Steinfeld flipped a switch on his machine. A spiral appeared in her thoughts, and when she opened her eyes, the spiral was still hanging in front of her. The coil moved towards her and engulfed her consciousness. Waves of energy pulsed through her brain like music as a cascade of emotions and memories washed through her body. Rebecca's hands twitched with surges of energy, and her chest hummed with subtle vibrations. Light flashes went off behind her eyes, and she felt euphoric.

And just like that, she was back in her familiar reality. Baby Alex sat at his table, playing with geometric shapes, while Anastasios watched over him.

"Anastasios." Rebecca's voice crackled through her scraped vocal cords.

Her husband looked over at her and rushed to her side. "Rebecca, you're conscious. How do you feel? Can you understand me?"

"Why wouldn't I be able to understand you, love?"

Anastasios paused and stared at her: "So you don't you remember what happened? The doctors said that might be the case."

"I'm not sure what you're talking about, but you're a sight for sore eyes. I had a strange experience. I'll tell you about it in a minute. I'm so glad to be back home," Rebecca said.

Anastasios shook his head, a confused expression on his face. "Rebecca, you never left home, you've been in a coma for months. It happened suddenly. One minute you were playing with the baby and the next minute, you were unconscious."

"So that's how I appeared to you? In a coma?"

"Yes, I was frightened you'd never wake up. The doctors couldn't find anything wrong with you. It was like the coma Regina went into after Alex exhaled the gas cloud in the hospital."

Anastasios brought her a glass of water. "You said something happened to you? Do you mean a dream?"

"Not exactly." She told Anastasios about her reality-two experiences. He lowered his head and looked at the floor after she'd finished.

"You don't believe me," Rebecca said.

"Yes, I do, love. But we need to see the doctor to talk about what happened to you."

"What date is it?"

Anastasios raised his eyebrows: "It's December 31st. Why?"

"Tomorrow I'll prove to you that everything I told you is true."

"Get some rest, and I'll take the baby to play with his friends. The nurse will bring you anything you need; just ask her," Anastasios said.

Rebecca frowned. Things must have been bad for her husband to hire a nurse to take care of her. "Thank you, love, for keeping me safe."

Anastasios turned to her with a poignant smile. "I'd do anything for you."

The following day, Rebecca woke up after a refreshing sleep. She wasn't sure when Alexandros would try to reach her telepathically and wandered around the house to distract herself. They were eating lunch when it happened. The voice in her head wasn't dramatic or loud, but it was authoritative. The effect was remarkably like a mobile phone held to her ear. "Rebecca, can you hear me?" reality two Alexandros mind spoke.

She wasn't sure what to do or say in front of Anastasios and baby Alex. "Yes," she mind spoke.

"Do you have a problem talking to me now?" Alexandros mind spoke.

"No, I was expecting you. Please tell me what happened to my alter ego in reality two," Rebecca mind spoke.

"Her treatment for schizophrenia was finally successful. The clinic released her yesterday and she was reunited with her parents," Alexandros answered.

"So soon?"

"Remember, time passes faster in my reality compared to yours," Alexandros mind spoke.

She fought a surreal feeling. How was she going to explain all of this to Anastasios? She looked at her husband. "Love, I'm mind speaking now with Alexandros in reality two."

Anastasios put his fork down slowly: "Prove it," he said.

"How? What type of proof will convince you?"

"Give me details about the machine he's using to communicate with you."

Reality two Alexandros described the main details of how the machine worked and she explained it to Anastasios,

259

who had to suspend his disbelief. There was no way she could know those technical details. Rebecca had never been talented with machines and even found it difficult to work an oven.

"So, what does reality two Alexandros want?" Anastasios said, still perplexed.

"He wants to help us with technologies to heal cancer and other wondrous things. Reality two Alexandros has invented machines to enhance our psychological powers," Rebecca said. "In his reality, scientists and ordinary people can communicate freely with the consciousness of people whose loved ones have died. Can you imagine what a comfort it would be to continue communicating with their souls after they transform?"

"It doesn't sound possible. I mean, how will he send this complicated information?" Anastasios said.

"To transfer his knowledge through me, he needs a mind projector," Rebecca said.

"How will this work? You don't have a scientist's knowledge. How will he communicate through you if you can't understand what he's teaching us?"

"That's a good question. We need to project your thoughts onto a physical screen so that other scientists can see them," Alexandros mind spoke.

"I doubt that we have the technology you need. I can speak to the science department at the university and to my friend Sam. He's a physicist. Make quantum contact again in two days," Rebecca mind spoke.

The voice in her mind went quiet, and she prayed that reality two Alexandros would come back. Her colleagues in the science department told her that there were already experiments on thought projection technology. The machine was in development, but it would take several decades to finish. Two days later, she heard Alexandros' distinct voice in her mind and told him she'd found out about the technology he wanted them to create.

"Rebecca, write down exactly what I'm about to tell you. Pass it on to your colleagues so they can build the mind projection technology quicker," he mind spoke.

She wrote his instructions quickly as they streamed through her consciousness. Although they were meaningless to her, when she showed them to the university's scientists, the simplicity of the design and software needed to project thoughts onto a screen astonished them. They worked fast on a prototype once she explained why she needed it.

The university board of directors was quick to back the new research. After all, Rebecca and Anastasios had helped them to overcome Varhaan's hostile takeover and the university was going from strength to strength. Rebecca persuaded them by describing the mind projection technology in enough detail and assuring them that the scientists could build the machine fast.

Chapter 16

Rebecca's friend Sam led the team of scientists that built the Alexandros Machine in less than six months. They hoped to open a line of communication in the collective consciousness between reality two Alexandros and their scientists.

For the time being, Rebecca was the only person who was quantum entangled with Alexandros in reality two, so she was the first person to project his thoughts onto a massive screen in a purpose-built laboratory at the university.

It was D-day, the moment they would find out whether the Alexandros Machine worked to connect different realities in time and space. Rebecca lay flat on a white cushioned bed and stared at the silver ceiling, where the first mind projections from reality 2 would appear on a high-resolution screen. Her stomach cramped with nerves. The communication between Alexandros and Rebecca wasn't always reliable, given how easily disrupted entanglement could be. Rebecca closed her eyes and touched her bracelet to calm down.

"Open your eyes, Rebecca, I've found it makes the machine work better," reality two Alexandros mind spoke.

The familiar sound of his voice in her head made her smile.

"Are you ready?" he said.

"Yes."

The machine hummed behind her head. Immediately, a rapid stream of plans, blueprints, formulae, and pages of text flashed in front of her eyes. A millisecond later, they appeared on the screen in her reality. The three scientists behind her took a collective breath as the information poured onto the screen's shiny surface.

"It's wondrous!" Sam said amid a chorus of gasps and exclamations from the other scientists. Right before their eyes, a treasure trove of knowledge and enlightenment streamed onto the screen, recorded all the while by special equipment.

Here were machines that cured cancer without side-effects. Neural network instruments that could heal Alzheimer's and a host of other deadly and devastating brain diseases. The Alexandros Machine promised to expand into a new event horizon of human potential.

"Rebecca, that's enough for now; this could be dangerous for you," Alexandros mind spoke. Her whole body felt drained of energy, and she barely had enough strength to mind-speak: 'goodbye for now.' Alexandros' voice faded as quickly as her consciousness.

To be continued.

Coming soon! 'The Soul Tracker', the sequel to 'The Light Walker'.

Read the beginning of 'The Soul Tracker'.

Chapter 1

When Rebecca woke up at home, Anastasios told her that two days had passed: "I thought you'd gone back into a coma," he said, gripping her hand. She looked around to see her familiar things, grateful her consciousness hadn't split again.

"Did it work? Is the information recorded and complete?" Rebecca said.

"Yes, your colleagues said they could start working on the technologies soon. They're hopeful they'll begin curing cancer within a year," Anastasios said. "The university is delighted and plans to offer you tenure and your own department."

"That's amazing news. I must get up and go to work," Rebecca said.

Anastasios chuckled. "Hold your horses, it can wait for a day. I told Sam you'd be in tomorrow."

Rebecca subsided back into bed. "Yes, thank you. That's probably best. I still feel woozy. Did Alexandros give us the technology to connect consciousness to consciousness?"

"I'm not sure. Sam didn't talk to me about it, not that it means anything, since all the project's information is confidential. If you ask me, it's too early for us to have such power and access to other people's minds."

Rebecca gave Anastasios a hug. "You could be right, love. Alexandros was always a wise old soul. I can't wait to see what miracles we'll accomplish with his technology."

It was the beginning of a new era in parapsychological technology, but Rebecca had no idea of what was to come.

Follow Sarah Fenwick's Author page on Amazon.com and stay updated with her new releases!

https://www.amazon.com/stores/Sarah-Fenwick/author/B08P8L2L3G

Acknowledgements

Thanks to the pioneers of consciousness theory, Dr. Carl Jung and to the other visionaries mentioned in this book who see beyond the façade of reality: J.J. McFadden, William James, Dr. Joseph Bank Rhine and Uri Geller.

Gratitude to Geoff Fenwick for his support during the editing process, and thanks go to Zoe Georgallides and Anna Roy for lunches, brainstorming and beta reading. Encouragement kudos to Jane Fenwick and the whole family who believe in my writing.

Thanks to you, dear reader, for supporting my work.

Sarah Fenwick